Sun and Sand

Center Point
Large Print

Also by Max Brand® and available from
Center Point Large Print:

Jingo
The Winged Horse
The Cure of Silver Cañon
The Red Well
Lightning of Gold
Daring Duval
Sour Creek Valley
Gunfighters in Hell

**This Large Print Book carries the
Seal of Approval of N.A.V.H.**

Sun and Sand

A Western Trio

MAX BRAND®

CENTER POINT LARGE PRINT
THORNDIKE, MAINE

The text of this Large Print edition is unabridged.
In other aspects, this book may vary
from the original edition.
Printed in the United States of America
on permanent paper.
Set in 16-point Times New Roman type.

ISBN: 978-1-68324-899-6 (hardcover)
ISBN: 978-1-68324-903-0 (paperback)

Library of Congress Cataloging-in-Publication Data

Names: Brand, Max, 1892-1944, author.
Title: Sun and sand : a western trio / Max Brand®.
Description: Center Point Large Print edition. | Thorndike, Maine :
    Center Point Large Print, 2018.
Identifiers: LCCN 2018019220| ISBN 9781683248996
    (hardcover : alk. paper) | ISBN 9781683249030
    (paperback : alk. paper)
Subjects: LCSH: Large type books. | GSAFD: Western stories.
Classification: LCC PS3511.A87 A6 2018 | DDC 813/.52—dc23
LC record available at https://lccn.loc.gov/2018019220

Contents

The Flaming Rider

In 1928 Frederick Faust published ten serials and eleven short novels in the pages of Street & Smith's *Western Story Magazine*. Additionally a five-part serial appeared in *Far West Illustrated*. "The Flaming Rider" appeared in the December 29th issue of *Western Story Magazine* under Faust's Peter Henry Morland byline. It is an Indian story in which heavy betting on a horse race inevitably leads to tension at the newly established Fort Meany where large groups of Cheyennes, Blackfeet, and Crows have gathered to trade their goods. This is the story's first appearance since its original publication.

I

This happened when Fort Meany was one year old.

For forty years, Henry Meany had trapped and hunted and traded before he decided to build his fort, and then he drew on all his experience in order to select a perfect place.

He did not want the headwaters of some large stream, up which rivals would come with their keelboats and undersell him. He simply wanted wood and water and a strategic position in relation to the buffalo on the one hand and the Indians on the other. So he selected a bend of the Little Silver and hurried up the walls of his fort. They were erected of sod, cut thick, of course, and wet down to make them solid—wet down, and tamped, but at the best not very satisfactory walls.

On the outside, those walls were surfaced with ten- and twelve-foot saplings, fixed deeply in the earth, and giving a sheer face above the reach of a horseman. The mound rose a little above this, and there was ample room on top for a man to walk at ease, or to lie prone and shoot with his rifle through the grooves that were sunk in the upper surface of the mound.

Inside of this thick, clumsy wall there were

rude shelters made of logs, of buffalo hides, or of more turf, stretching around in a circle. Inside of those shelters were the goods of the traders, and, usually cached deep in the cellar rooms, the proceeds of the thriving trade with the Indians.

Free traders were welcome. Those who hauled goods down from the river could, if they chose, sell out at a certain price to Henry Meany. Or, on the other hand, they were permitted to stay, enjoying the advantages of the wood and the water at the fort and of the concourse of Indians who were fairly sure to resort there, lured by the ancient fame of Henry Meany and his fair dealing. In this case, it was expected that they should pay down to the fort a proportion of their profits, ranging from ten to five percent. Actually the percentage was less, for if Henry Meany took one of ten buffalo robes, he did not see to it that his selection was one of the best.

For all these reasons, the pool of merchandise that collected there at the beginning of the season was large and rich; the traders kept trekking south from the river, and the Indians, lured by the report of "big doings", began to sweep in from all directions. There were so many of them that they promised to load down the traders with robes and furs. And, therefore, another caravan was not unwelcome.

Henry Meany in person, as was his custom, rode out to welcome it, his son attending him, and as soon as he saw the oxen in the distance, swaying across the prairie, he said to his son: "The captain of that outfit is a man of sense, Charlie. He's brought his animals through in fine condition."

Usually a few men galloped wildly ahead when a caravan of wagons came within sight of such a trading post, but the advance guard of this train moved with more dignity and finally showed as three typical scouts of the Western country.

The ponies of the riders accompanying the caravan moved softly at the Indian foxtrot, and rough as the horses appeared, the men were still rougher, and yet their costumes were fitted to their life. They wore coarse shirts, blue as a rule, and long coats of buckskin that fanned out at the bottom, so as to give the rider plenty of room in the saddle. Below the waist they were dressed like Indians, with leather trousers or leggings, and with moccasins on their feet. Some of them wore soft hats, always with wide, flopping brims that curled up and down as the wind struck them, while others had bits of cloth wrapped, Moorish fashion, around the head. These were young men, indifferent as Indians to the glare of the prairie sun.

These riders were equipped for the longest journey, almost always with a long, small-bore rifle kept in a case to protect it from the weather, and with knives, whetstones, pouches, and horns for bullets and powder, even with bullet molds, with leather wrapped around the handles.

The advance guard now approached the fort. On either side was a young man, and in the center was an imposing rider with silver hair flowing down over his shoulders or lifting gently in the wind. His face showed no more than middle age, but his features had the look of being hammered by time and weather, and his jaw was habitually locked in grim determination.

It was not a face easy to look into; the eyes rested upon it as upon a book that is sure to contain tales of wild adventures. One could feel the burn of the desert and the white sweep of the blizzard as he drew nearer; one could feel starvation, the exhaustion of endless marches, long seasons of watchfulness when every bush might hold an enemy. But though his hair was whitened, it somehow made him look only more fierce and formidable. One felt that here was a man who would be master of all situations.

When he came up to Meany, he raised his hand, in Indian salute, then, with a mutual murmur of pleasure, the two men shook hands.

The newcomer was William Duncan, long known to Meany, associated with him in many enterprises, and famous throughout the West. He was at home in the mountains, and a leader of mountain men. He was at home in the plains, and a leader in the more dangerous work there.

He was celebrated as trapper, hunter, scout, and Indian fighter. Men said that twenty brass tacks had been hammered into the stock of his rifle.

Duncan and Meany now drew back upon a hummock. The youngsters gave them respectful distance. Duncan began to smoke as the train went by. He took out a bowl of red stone, the famous pipestone of the Indian plainsman. He filled this with tobacco mixed with shreds of fragrant bark, fitted a long stem to the bowl, sprinkled powdered buffalo dung on top of the smoking mixture, and lighted the pipe with a shower of sparks from his flint and steel. These preparations were made without haste, and yet with the skilled speed of long practice.

"I've never seen cattle come in from the river looking fatter," said Meany.

Duncan blew a puff of smoke upon his hands, which he rubbed together. He blew another puff to the ground, directed a third toward the sky, and automatically passed the pipe to his companion.

Meany smiled faintly at the Indian ceremony through which Duncan was passing with such mechanical absent-mindedness, but he was careful to accept the pipe gravely, puff at it in the same fashion, and pass it back in exactly the same position in which he had received it. One never could tell. Every pipe had its special way to be smoked, and not even Meany could know to what extent the Indian superstitions of the plains had seized upon the individual trapper and trader.

"They're fatter cattle than I'll ever bring in again," said Duncan. "But I've had an anchor all the trip. I'm five days late. I've been anchored on the way." He said this with a gradually increasing heat.

Meany did not venture a remark; he continued to watch the oxen heaving past, leaning on their yokes, and swaying in clumsy unison. They were very slow, but the thrust of their weight had a resistless force far beyond that of a mule or a horse. By the size and condition of the animals, and by the manner in which they pulled and the sort of vehicle they were drawing, Meany could estimate almost to a hundredweight the burden of the cargo in every wagon.

"You're traveling heavy, though," he remarked to Duncan.

"I'm heavy with meat today," said Duncan. "I'm bringing in enough to fill the bellies of every man in the fort, and all the red men outside of it . . . even if they're forty-pound feasters."

Meany expressed his pleasure, for it was one of his hardest tasks to get in meat sufficient for food for all who surrounded the fort. The buffalo were constantly driven from the vicinity of the camp by random single hunters. His own hunting parties had to go to a great distance, kill the meat, jerk it, and cart it back. It cost time and money and only kept them in dry meat. This fresh supply was a godsend.

"But," said Duncan, "that's not the reason why I'm late. There . . . there's the reason," he broke out, and pointed far to the rear.

In that distance, Meany could see a wagon stagger over the edge of a hill and roll slowly down it, drawn by four animals in a motley group. "That wagon is falling over, man," he said.

"It's been falling these last four days," said Duncan with extreme bitterness, "but the shiftless fool has always said that he thought it would stand up until he got it to the fort. The load shifted crossing a creekbed four days ago, and it's been sagging over like that more and more every moment. Hang me, if it don't break my heart to see him get even this close to the fort with it."

"Who is it?" asked Meany, and immediately regretted the question, because it called a torrent of terrible curses from the captain of the caravan.

Finally intelligible words broke through the profanity. "It's a greenhorn! It's a tenderfoot jackass! It's a fool!" yelled Duncan.

"From the East, eh?"

"The farthest possible," said Duncan. "Where there's no knowledge that's worth a man knowing. A gambling, drunken, worthless, shiftless, grinning fool."

"How did he get out here?"

"His family sent him. The old story . . . no good at home, so let him go out and rot on the prairies. He'll begin to do so soon. He won't live five days in the fort. I hope some red man gets him. Reached Saint Louis with the price of five fine wagons, and the cattle to pull them. Reached upriver with the price of one, or less . . . gambled the rest away . . . gambles all the time . . . gambles for anything . . . gambles like an Indian. A useless, worthless idiot. Last man every morning to outspan. Last man in every evening. Always at the end of the line. Always the tail. Lord, but I've wanted to have the wringing of his throat. . . ." He stopped, spluttering.

"You should have cut him out and let him stay behind," said Meany grimly. "Puppies like that should be taught with a whip."

"You can't cut off a grinning half-wit," said Duncan. "Wait . . . you'll see."

II

The rest of the caravan went by as smoothly as the hands of a clock. So extraordinary was the discipline that stern Captain Duncan had imposed upon the members of the outfit that they did not press forward with any undue haste in drawing close to the fort, but went on in the same plodding manner in which they had gone across the plains.

Each driver or horseman turned and gave some sort of a salute to Meany and Duncan in passing, and then they went on, and the last wagon passed in that compact troop. The surface of the prairie was beginning to be chopped up and ground to pieces where the wheels had beaten through the upper crust, and every puff of wind now blew a cloud of dust away.

But still the wagon to the rear came slowly, slowly forward. In the distance, it seemed to progress hardly faster than the minute hand of a clock, and even when it drew much closer, it did no more than crawl across the surface of the plain.

There were several reasons for the slowness, and Meany took heed of them one by one. In the first place, wherever the wagon lurched, the wheels on one side lifted in dangerous fashion from the surface of the road, and the entire wagon threatened to pitch upon the other side. In the second place, the wagon itself was so old, and the wheels were set on at such varying and crazy angles, that each seemed to be taking a way of its own, or struggling to do so, and there was a terrible groaning as they strove to part company.

But the wagon and its behavior were nothing compared with the animals that drew the load. There was a tall, slab-sided steer on the near wheel, and a little dumpy, cream-colored cow

17

on the off. Before this span appeared a mule, gray with innumerable years, lofty, bearded with time, and sinking at the knees, and beside him staggered a two-year-old colt, gaunt and hump-backed with the labor. In the lead marched a shaggy Indian pony, with ears flattened, and nostrils sucked in with age, and beside it the team was completed by a burro hardly larger than a good-size dog.

Beside this strange assortment of working beasts walked a moon-faced half-breed, with the coloring of a smoky Indian and the lips and eyes of a Negro. He punched the six along with a red-tipped goad, and bellowed at them in a voice sometimes whining high and sometimes booming like thunder.

But to the windward, out of the dust, there appeared a young man on a beautiful thorough-bred. He sat to the side upon it, his back ungracefully bowed out, while he thrummed upon a guitar, and the sound of his voice came sweet and small with distance to the ears of Meany.

"Is that it?" asked Meany with something like awe.

Captain Duncan looked on his companion. He was speechless with rage. "Five days late," he managed to say at last. "I threatened to leave the fool behind me. He only laughed and seemed to think it was a joke. If the march had been a

18

hundred miles farther, I would have cut him from the outfit and let the Indian dogs chew his bones for supper. Look at him!"

This last of all the caravan, seeing the two beside the road, turned toward them at once, while Duncan went on: "Do you see? Yonder and yonder? Every day half a dozen or a dozen of those buzzards have been in the offing, ready to swoop down and eat up that laggard and his wagonload. And every day I've had to halt and wait . . . or send back an extra span to haul him into line. The whole caravan has suffered for that fool. The whole caravan. I wish that the redskins had picked him off. I can't imagine why they haven't."

Here and there, forms of Indians drifted, easily told by their position on their horses, their legs very high, and their bodies jutting forward, their backs rounded. It was a very clumsy position for riding at a jog or at a walk, but when the horses galloped, every Indian was in tune with it, like a jockey. It seemed evident that they were waiting for some accident to happen to the last of the wagons, and then, even so close to the fort, they would fly down and pick up what they could in the way of plunder, a coup or two, and perhaps a random scalp to dry over their fires.

But at last, seeing that Meany and Duncan were waiting for the laggard, they pulled to the right and to the left, as though at a signal, and suddenly disappeared in the rolling ground. The stranger, in the meantime, was gradually coming up to the two elders.

"And what's his name?" asked Meany.

"A good name and a good family . . . Tarlton. But you'll have a fool even in a palace, eh? They've shoveled him out, and here he is. I wouldn't trade him for a slave. I wouldn't trade him for the little finger of a slave. Cardsharp and pistol fighter! *Faugh!*"

Meany saw a handsome youngster of not more than twenty-five. Not that twenty-five was then particularly young in the West, where often a partisan would reach celebrity at such an age, but these fellows were young in years only, and had been hardened by a whole life on the prairie or in the mountains.

Tarlton, however, had obviously been sheltered. He had the open, careless eye that is the sign of long nurture; his skin was more pink than brown, in spite of the long journey across the plains, and his laughter as he came up with the two plainsmen was as freely flowing as the laughter of a child.

This misfit upon the plains wore riding trousers, a closely fitted jacket, and a scarf was wrapped about his throat—a *silken* scarf. There was no sign of a knife at his belt, no rifle balanced across the pommel of his saddle. The saddle itself was a light English pad equipped with two pistol holsters from which the handles protruded a little. This was his only armament.

Duncan stared at his companion, and Meany looked back at Duncan in disgust.

"And what do you mean by hanging back like that?" roared Duncan. "What do you . . . ?" Rage choked him. His stern face turned crimson and purple and became swollen with fury.

Young Tarlton saluted adroitly. "Sire," he said, "I am the rear guard of the grand army."

"You!" shouted Duncan. "You're the rear jackass of the entire world! Get out of my sight!"

"Men, retire by platoons," said Tarlton. He kept his hand at a long salute, and, still perched sidewise on the saddle, he forced the fine animal he was riding to traverse, and so gradually approached the staggering wagon ahead.

"He can ride," Duncan admitted as the strange outfit and its owner went reeling up the slight slope toward the fort, where the rest of the caravan was pooling before the entrance to the place. "He can ride well enough to shine in a park. But an Indian would send ten arrows through that fool and make him look like a porcupine, while he was showing off the paces of his horse."

"Did he bring that horse all the way up the river?"

"By Jiminy," said Duncan, "he did exactly that. And not only all the way up the river, but all the way from Virginia, also. Man, think of

21

that horse when the first cold weather blows up. Think of that skin like silk, when even the Indian ponies that look more like bears than horses are shuddering and shaking, and drawing up their bellies with the cold."

"He ain't the first bit of an old family that has been turned into buzzard food," said Meany. "And the way I figger it, Duncan, out in this part of the world, them of us that get on have got to climb a ladder of bones. He's another rung or two, and that's all. But I've never seen a better horse. I've never seen a slicker mover than that."

"If he ain't grained once a day," said Duncan bitterly, "he's dropping his head and losing his heart. I'd rather have a cat to ride than a silken worthless fool like that horse. We'll go on toward the fort. I've got a jug in my wagon, and it's not filled with trade whiskey. It's got bourbon in it that will wash the dust out of your throat and out of your brain at the same time."

They rode on, side-by-side, until they came to the last hill before the fort, with young Charlie Meany and Duncan's escort reining well to the rear. Here Meany halted for a moment and pointed to the Indian encampment. In three broad sections they surrounded the fort with the whiteness of their teepees. On the river edge, parties of boys were playing, women were carrying up water to the lodges, and young men raced their ponies over the plains.

Duncan viewed this approvingly. "What have you got here?" he asked. "That's Piegan, I'd say."

"That's Piegan," agreed Meany.

"Beaver?"

"They've come down with the best of the Blackfoot country in their packs. They've got everything in the shape of a plew from the mountains to Fort Union, and from Belly River to the Yellowstone. They've brought them down here, and they're reaching for trade. Their axes are wore out or lost. Their knives have been sharpened away till they'd bend in a thick wind. Their beads are broken, or lost, or used up. Their blankets are rags, and they've got a hunger for tea and coffee and sugar in the bottom of their bellies. Man, man, there's the making of ten fortunes in that outfit of Piegans. I tell you, there's riches untold in the packs of those Blackfeet."

Duncan regarded the teepees with a broad, mirthless grin, and his thin nostrils quivered and expanded.

"Cheyennes?" he said, waving to the right-hand side of the river at the smallest encampment.

"Loaded to back-breaking with pemmican and robes. No better robes than the Cheyenne squaws cure. They've brought in painted ones by the score . . . and deerskin suits covered with quill work and beadwork. And they're as hungry for trade as the Piegans, pretty nigh."

"And what are those?"

"Horse-stealing Crows. With plenty of pelts. And ready to trade, too."

"Aye," said Duncan, "there's a fortune in those teepees, yonder, but, by my way of thinking, you've got three tribes of the hardest-fighting Indians in the world stacked around your little fort, Meany."

III

All remarks that Duncan had to make were listened to with the greatest attention, and Meany hastened to take the great partisan into the fort and point out his preparations for defense. Looking east and looking west upon the walls of the fort, there were little brass howitzers, and from a barrel Meany picked up a handful of small slugs to show with what the cannon were loaded. The flash and the boom of them could be depended upon to turn any Indian charge, he was sure. Duncan nodded with approval, but he pointed out that the day when the explosion of the cannon was looked upon by the Indians as a miraculous thunder was passing.

He seemed more pleased with other arrangements, the chief of which was a device for instantly closing the heavy gate, which was covered with a double or treble layer of massive bulls' hides, strong enough to turn bullets unless they were fired close up and at exactly the right angle. With the gate closed, there were pockets on all the walls, high up, known only to him, to his son, and to two very trusted men. In case the Indians who freely entered the fort should start a disturbance, the gate easily could be closed by means of the powerful levers that were attached to it, and Meany and the other leaders could call their best men to the walls, to which they were instructed to follow. There, even if they had no weapons at the moment in their hands, they readily could find the caches of well-kept and loaded rifles, and, with these, they could control any number of wranglers in the interior of the fort, or be prepared at need to beat off a charge from without.

"You've got everything ready," agreed Duncan, "unless the game is played against you with a joker."

Meany nodded. He knew, as every other frontier trader knew, that until his fort became much larger and better defended than it was at present, it would be impossible to keep it against a resolute assault in such numbers as the Indians were able to muster. Every fort was in danger of being wiped out every trading season, but the traders clung to their work. The profits were big, and if one fort in three was wiped out, that was charged to the account of "loss" and the business went on. Human life was not counted, in adding up the bills of the frontier.

When Duncan had been conducted over the fort in detail, however, his gloomy face became more tranquil. From the western rampart he looked out at the stretch of plain, where the numerous caravans that could not be included in the fort were arranged each in its own ring. They looked defenseless enough, but Meany pointed out that he himself had insisted that a strong guard be maintained in each of these caravans day and night. While that was done, they made powerful outworks to the fort itself, a wagon fort being no child's play to be carried.

Duncan looked back inside at the few Indians who were sauntering here and there in the fort, all with empty hands. He looked out at the swarming throngs on the grass of the prairie.

"When does the trading begin?" he asked.

"Whenever the big chiefs can agree on the rates of sale," said Meany.

"And what do they want?"

"Spotted Calf is down here with the Piegans. He's reasonable enough. A cupful of sugar for a fine buffalo robe is his price. And other things in proportion. One could get on with that sort of a scale."

Duncan looked deliberately at the speaker, and a slow smile spread upon his face. Infinite greed sparkled in his eyes. "Is that the way of it?" he asked a little huskily.

Meany smiled in turn. "That would be the way with the Blackfeet, and all their robes, and their beaver. But Little Bull is up here with the Cheyennes, and he has different ideas. He wants a quart of sugar, at least. And other things on the same scale."

It was an early day in trading, and still prices were as absurd as this, but Duncan scowled as he listened. It was not large profits that he wanted, it was a fortune, and the greater the fortune, the more logical that he should win it.

"I never knew anything but trouble to come out of Cheyennes," he said. "Can you keep off the Cheyennes and trade with the Blackfeet?"

"Not without starting a war between them."

"Which way would the Crows jump?"

"I don't know. The three of 'em hate each other's hearts, anyway. Suppose the Crows should go against the Cheyennes. There are a few Pawnees in with the Crows, and that would turn the whole lot."

"Aye," said Duncan. "Three Pawnees would poison a whole nation against the Cheyennes. Why, it would be a good thing to let the fight come, charge into the middle of it, and help the Crows and the Blackfeet to take scalps. I'm getting to be an old man, and I need a little skirmishing to make me feel young again."

"Oh, aye," said Meany. He patted the stock of his rifle. The head of brass tacks glimmered in it like wicked little yellow eyes. "Yes, yes," he said. "There's a place for fighting, but not at a fort. We build forts to keep out of war, eh? Not to have trouble."

Duncan sighed even while he nodded. "It's true," he said. "If you start with a battle at your first trading, there'll always be suspicion and the fort will have a bad name. We have to start Fort Meany right. And how, then? Why, to make terms, to make terms. Have you tried a present to Little Bull?"

"I gave him a paint horse that his mouth was watering over," said Meany. "But it didn't change him. He's like a baby. The more you give him, the more he wants. I gave him the horse, and he asked where was the saddle to put on its back."

"Well?"

"I gave him the saddle, and he asked where was the rifle to balance across the pommel of it, and the pouch of shot and the horn of powder."

Duncan snorted in fury. "Something tells me that the hair is sitting loose on the head of that Indian," he said.

The teeth of Meany clicked in equal anger. "I had to swallow it and say nothing," he said. "And now he's holding up the start of the trade. The Indians get restless. I don't know. Another few days and some of the bucks may begin to

28

drift off. Mine is not the only fort in the land. And there are a pair of 'breeds up here from the American Fur Company, ready to persuade the whole crowd over to their place."

Duncan groaned with vexation. "They're getting ready for a race," he pointed out. "Let's go there and watch. There's no better way to mix around among the braves. Take along some sugar and whiskey. Give a cupful here and there among the chiefs. Tell them that Little Bull is a great chief, but that he doesn't understand trading. I know some of those Piegans, too, or I'm unlucky. We'll see what we can do."

So they started out together, and their young men followed them, not obviously as a body-guard, but always lingering in the rear, anxious to watch the tactics of their elders, trailing in to listen to snatches of conversation, and always with their long rifles ready.

At the gate a girl of twenty, dressed in neatly fitted deerskin, bright with beadwork and quill work, and riding a gray pony with beads braided into its long mane, swept up to them. She was Meany's daughter Helen. Could she go out to see the races?

Duncan looked at Meany, and Meany looked at Duncan. There was always danger in a crowd such as that yonder on the plain. And yet, as Meany pointed out in a murmur, it might prove to the Indians the friendship of the trader, if he trusted his daughter in the throng. So it was agreed.

"Whatever you do, never get out of my sight," said Meany. "Never ride fast. Keep your horse in hand. Never meet the eye of any buck. Look at the women, pat the children on the head. Give a few beads around. You can talk a little Piegan. If you see a squaw that looks like a chief's wife, talk to her, find out the name of her husband, and tell her how famous he is."

The girl nodded, laughed, and was instantly gone through the gate, with most of these instructions vanished from her brain before she was outside the fort.

Meany called to his son.

"Have you let Helen go out?" the boy asked gloomily as he came up.

"I have. You follow her. Take Rixon, over yonder. Follow her close."

"I can follow her," said the brown-faced youngster, "but I dunno that I can follow her eyes. She's mighty free with 'em."

"Do what you're told, and save your talk for afterward."

So Charles Meany went out to trail his sister through the throng, and with him he took a long, loose-jointed son of toil—Rixon, the trapper, a man of war.

Just beyond the gates were the circles of the wagons, but beyond the wagons the plain was covered with Indians, and the water of the little river was continually dashed to white as hasty riders galloped through from side to side.

It was the prime of the year. The prairies were covered with fresh green. The shaggy winter coats of the ponies were gone, in many cases, which left the little animals shining with sweat and with velvet. Others were patched over like mangy buffalo, and still others resolutely clung to their winter coats, long and wolfish.

But the blood was stirring in horse and man. The wind was fresh and sweet with the scent of the grass, crushed by thousands of hoofs in the hollow and on the hills. The sound of the voices was deep with the words of men, and bright with the chatter of the women, and the thin, high notes of the children, and always a minor tone floated in the air where an infant was crying.

When Duncan and Meany came up, they found that a distance had been cleared along the bank of the stream, where the ground was perfectly level. Two heaps of sod had been put up some hundred and fifty yards apart. The races were to be run around these.

And now two ponies were prepared—a Piegan and a Crow were ready for the start. Every Piegan voice was offering a bet on his nation's representative, and every Crow was offering a bet on the Crow.

"Hello, Meany," said Duncan. "Helen, there, has found out the tail of my caravan."

31

IV

Looking through the tossing throng of hands, of passing horses, Henry Meany saw that his daughter Helen was at the side of young Tarlton, but her attention was not for him alone. It streamed forth over the entire crowd of men and women and children. Her smile shone from the distance, and the long massive braids of her hair glimmered like polished copper as she turned here and there. Her head was never quiet, and neither was her hand.

"She's found something new," said Meany. "Darned if she ain't always finding something new. What's old is dull for her. What's new is beautiful."

"Even a new fool?"

"It looks that way. But how's she to know the freak?"

"By the talk of him, and the fool look in his face," said the stern partisan. "We'd better go down and listen to him."

They advanced as the Indians bet right and left. There is nothing that an Indian man loves so much as any game of chance. Now, with sparkling eyes, they offered blankets, beaver skins worth $6 each, even knives and guns, bows and arrows. The horses themselves were stripped of saddles and offered in the risk, and sometimes the full panoply of horse and saddle, and bull-skin shield, and long lance, bow, and filled quiver.

There was not much arguing about values at that moment. It was anything to make a bet as big as could be afforded, and make it quickly before the race began. For every Indian was confident that the race would go to his representative. What matter, then, if he offered a bet twice the size of that of his adversaries? Soon all would be in his possession.

"This is good work," said Meany. "It will loosen them up. It will pile a lot of goods in the hands of half as many Indians as had them before. And then they'll be ready for fast trading, and cheap trading."

"That's not true," Duncan declared. "The more an Indian has, the more he wants. Your poor beggar of a brave is generous. He'd give you his skin. A rich chief would make a fat living in Jerusalem."

"Or Scotland," suggested Meany.

Duncan accepted this reference to his nationality with a broad grin.

"The more they have, the more they want," insisted Duncan, and Meany did not deny the truth of this.

The excitement was growing high. The warriors, conscious that they were the center of attraction, were parading their ponies up and down the line, and each of them made a speech at the same time. Each announced that he trusted in his pony, that it never had been fairly beaten, that the Sky People would give it speed this day, and invited friends to show their friendship by betting a little more on his chances.

In the midst of this growing noise and excitement, Meany and Duncan arrived at the place where the girl was at the side of young Tarlton— in time to hear him exchanging words with a Blackfoot who was calmly suggesting that the white man should give him the bright scarf around his neck, because he had a squaw in his teepee who would like to have it.

And Tarlton answered with perfect good nature, gravely assuring the Blackfoot in his own tongue that nothing could give him more pleasure than to bestow such a gift upon him, and that it was really for this purpose that he had come across the plains, but, that having come such a distance for such a purpose, he could not dream of letting the matter stand with such a paltry gift as this. However, the very cockles of his heart would be warmed by persuading the chief to accept a more splendid gift, which he would bring to him on another day.

Meany listened most intently to this conversation with a good deal of amazement.

"How's this, Duncan?" he asked. "I've never

heard a greenhorn talk bang-up smooth Blackfoot like this before."

"Every idle man has plenty of time to learn one thing," said Duncan. "While the *men* were on the boat, watching the banks and talking to the pilot, this blockhead spent his time talking with the half-breed Blackfoot that he has along with him, and he wrote down words, and memorized 'em, until you see how he can talk. The same way on the prairies. The *men* went out to throw a few buffalo and an antelope, now and then, while this fellow stayed behind with the half-breed and chattered Indian rot. D'you know the best that can come of him? A squawman. He'd shed his fine feathers and be glad of it, if he could find a woman to keep him."

"He's turned down the chief, however," said Meany. "He's learned the language, and he's learned the tune that the words go to, as well. Helen enjoyed that show."

For Helen Meany was laughing until she swayed in the saddle, and young Tarlton was laughing in turn as the frontiersmen came up to him.

"Now," said Duncan to the youth, "here's your chance to show what that high-priced mare is worth. Her legs are twice as long as the legs of those ponies. Why not try her in a race against 'em?"

"It's not a race. It's a dodging contest," said

Tarlton. "She'd barely get her legs stretched before she came to a turn."

"It's the sort of race that they have in this country," said Duncan. "And what's the good of a mare like that? She can't travel across country, because she's not strong enough to carry a man and a pack, and she can't win a race for you because her legs are too long for the turns. If I had a critter like that, Tarlton, I'll tell you what I'd do . . . I'd fat her up, and give the boys a feast."

Tarlton ran his thumb down the mare's sleek side. "She'd probably make good eating, at that," he admitted. "Wouldn't you, Camille?"

"Which?" snorted Meany.

"She's a French lady," explained Tarlton gravely.

"She runs to legs," commented Duncan scornfully. "She's apt to break up like pipe stems, if you get her among the rocks."

"You never can tell a sword until you've tried it," said Tarlton.

"A rifle ball will make the best sword in the world as foolish as a paper knife," retorted Meany.

"One can't have everything," Tarlton said. "Some things are useful. Some things are beautiful. And there you are."

In a dexterous fashion, his eye included Helen Meany in this remark, so that the girl flushed.

"Then make a picture of her and stick it in your pocket," said Duncan.

"Who can paint her eye and her mind?" Tarlton asked with a gesture.

"*Bah!*" Meany snorted.

But his daughter looked on the youth with a whimsical smile of understanding.

However, at that moment the two ponies were lined up for the race. There seemed such a vast difference between the two champions that the white men had bet to a man on the Blackfoot champion. This was a slender-limbed pony with the build and the head of a deer, and a lithe youth was on its back, a mere featherweight of a boy. On the other hand, the representative of the Crows was a thick-legged creature still wearing its shaggy winter coat. It had the neck of a ewe and the eye of a goat, red-stained and wicked. On its back was a huge brave of middle age, his legs dangling far toward the ground, and in his hand a massive club with a knotted head. However, the course was short, and the weight of the riders would not make a very great difference.

Frantic betting was the rule for the last moment before the start, and then a steady pressure from the rear as those behind strove to get in better position to view the race. The signal fell, and away darted the champions.

It was exactly as one would have guessed. Running like a deer, the Blackfoot pony stretched a length or more into the lead, and doubled this advantage by a lightning turn at the first corner. And at the second heap of turf there was still more daylight between it and the Crow pony.

But now the warrior roused himself. He began to swing his club, while the horse, shaking its head at every blow, strained forward, and the Crows filled the air with a roar of excitement. With all this effort, however, the Crow horse could not lessen the distance between it and the leader until they came to the third and last turn of the short race. Then it seemed as though the Blackfoot faltered and hung in its stride, for they flashed around the turf pile exactly even and rushed for home.

High the brave swung the club, whacking the sides of the Crow pony. Its shaggy legs flew; its stride increased, and the Blackfoot pony, suffering under the lash, ridden beautifully by the youngster with desperate, straining face, fell back inch by inch. His nose was at the shoulder of the Crow at the finish, and a long yell went up from the multitude, like the shout of ten thousand Indians charging for battle.

Then the noise died down.

The winners were too proud to show any exultation as they accepted the payment of the debts that had been made against them. The white men and the Blackfeet were too proud to show any anger. For a moment this quiet lasted, very strangely, and then the muttering of the losing Blackfeet began, one to another. The higher voices of the exulting Crows could be heard.

The whole crowd was in confused movement again, but this time it was milling around like cattle undetermined where to go. Their blood was up, and they wanted more of the same excitement—the loser's revenge, the winners more taste of victory.

This feeling of an unspoken challenge did not last long, because a ripple ran through the crowd. Among the Cheyennes there was a famous red stallion—swift as the wind, it was said, undefeated in races. It was the property of a great chief. He was bringing it in person to challenge the Crow.

And yonder he came, the stallion burning like copper beneath the sun, and the chief with a flutter of feathers in his hair. Toward him went the Crow, looking more like a caricature than ever on his goat-like horse.

V

Even the patriotism of the Cheyennes, the fame of their chief, and the beauty of his red bay stallion, however, could not induce them to bet as freely as the Blackfeet had done against the Crow's ragged pony. That ugly beast had proved its worth; many a Blackfoot now was "folding his arms over an empty stomach," as Spotted Calf, the Piegan chief, feelingly declared. And the Cheyennes took warning.

However, they gave their leader some support. Those whose horses had been beaten by the little stallion still felt that he must possess a measure of invincibility, and they brought out their beaver skins and their robes to the wagering. So the two were brought to the start and off they went. As before, the shaggy little brute of the Crows hung close during the first round, but with the second he turned into a distinct lead, for he dodged around the turf piles like a rabbit. He had the advantage of a very weatherly ship, which can easily cut close to the wind.

Headed for home on the last stretch, he had a three-length advantage. The Cheyennes were silent, and the Crows were sending up a jubilant yell when the rider of the bay stallion made up his mind to a desperate adventure.

Straight across the course ran a shallow draw in which water ran for a few days in the heaviest season of rainfall. Toward the river and farther back from it, its sides presented no obstacle whatever, so that on the outward stretch the horses dipped into the slight depression and swept easily out of it again. But in the back stretch the case was different. Here the draw had cut through a bank so that on the farther side—as the horses approached it—the bank rose almost sheer, six feet in height.

In order to avoid this, the racers had to swing out to a considerable distance, and now the Cheyenne determined to try to cut across the chord of the arc by driving straight across the draw. He sent the red bay down into the depression. A wild yell of astonishment from the Cheyennes and of fear from the Crows followed this maneuver. For an instant, the head of the stallion was seen to appear above the nearer bank, and then he toppled back.

The Crow pony went on to a hollow victory, and the Cheyenne chief rode out of the draw, covered with dust, and rode furiously back among his people.

It was at this moment, as the first yell of the Crows died down and the flourish of debt payments was completed, that Duncan said to Tarlton: "Now, my boy, if your mare is worth her salt, take her out and bring down the pride of the Crows a little."

Tarlton, with a shrug of his shoulders, answered: "What's the honor, after all, in beating a tired little pony?"

Duncan went off in disgust, but there was another who passed by almost unnoticed in the excitement of the crowd, and that was Little Bull—that noted Cheyenne chief who held up for terms four times as high as those which would have satisfied the Blackfeet in the trading. The reason for his demands was that he knew something of the whites and their ways; he even possessed a very sound knowledge of English speech, and for one instant he lingered in his stride to hear.

He went off with a light in his eye, for there was one thing that he did not understand, and that was the white man's banter, which falls somewhere between truth and an outright lie.

In the meantime, events were happening that were to give a new point to that random remark of young Tarlton, for Duncan and Meany, riding side-by-side, came through the press to where the triumphant Crow was surrounded by the envy and the admiration of his people. The warrior saw the trader and greeted him with a broad grin. Were there no horses among those of the white men which would give his pony a race?

"Yonder," said Meany, "you'll find a young man with a horse as fast as the Thunderbird that flies down the sky on three flaps of his wings. He will ride against your pony if you challenge him hard enough. Besides, he has enough wealth with him to fill two teepees to the crossing of the poles."

The Crow heard, and his eyes flashed a greedy fire. So he was presently twisting his way through the crowd until he reached Tarlton, who had been obligingly described by Meany in leaving. He found that young man engaged in telling Helen Meany why he had come to the West, and that conversation was of such interest that they sat their horses close together, stirrup to stirrup, and eye to eye. His account of how his original stake furnished by his father on leaving the East had shrunk in coming up the river made her gasp and made her laugh. And Tarlton laughed with her, and suddenly made the great, stern, mysterious prairies, where Indian dangers and Indian craft were born, seem to the girl a place of ridiculous pleasure and ridiculous beauty. One could not help laughing at the delightful face of this kind world. Young David Tarlton made the burden of all its worries a mere feather-weight.

In the midst of this chatter, a passage opened to them through the crowd, and the Crow appeared, and raised his hand in greeting to the boy. At his first words, Helen Meany cried out: "He offers to race you, because he hears you have a famous horse!"

Tarlton grinned at her. "Have you the tongue of a Blackfoot?" he said in that language.

"I have two tongues," replied the Crow, "one of them is the tongue of a Blackfoot, and both tongues speak the thing that is true. I have heard that your horse is as fast as the Thunderbird, which flies across the sky with three strokes of his wings. I have only an ugly pony, but today he has won, his heart is a big heart, and he would run even after a bird."

"Brother," said Tarlton, "it is true that this mare is a fast runner, but she steps with a long step. The eagle cannot dodge like the hawk. What would she do with her long legs in rounding the marks?"

"But in the straight run, she will bound like an eagle on the wind."

"Well," said Tarlton, "when she has learned the feel of this grass under her feet, she may try her luck. But not today."

The Crow sneered. He was a brave with scalps in his teepee and all of them had not the black hair of Indians. He said: "If my brother is afraid, we will run our horses for pleasure to feel the wind in our faces. We will not make a bet. My brother is young. Perhaps he has not many horses to risk?"

Tarlton flushed and started in his saddle. And the words came ringing off his tongue. "The horse I ride, and the saddle I ride on . . . the pistols in these pouches, and the bullets that go with them, against your horse, and your rifle, and your saddle, friend. And if you will double the distance, I'll double the stake."

The Crow looked. The mare was beautiful, to be sure, yet his own horse was a proved champion, and his rifle shot straight, but on the handles of the pistols he saw the bright golden chasing, and

44

his heart leaped. He never had seen such a thing before. Pistols, he knew, were weapons of war, but never had he beheld weapons so beautiful.

The bargain was made; their hands had closed on it before the girl could interfere, and the Crow was off toward the start with a malicious grin of triumph on his face.

It was not the first well-bred horse that had been matched against Indian ponies in these dodging races around a double or a triple goal, and the Crow knew very well that the agile footwork of the Indian pony was almost sure to more than offset the longer stroke of the thoroughbred.

"There!" cried Helen Meany. "You've lost it all before the race begins!"

"I have," admitted Tarlton. "But . . . when I first saw these plains, I told myself that I would like to walk on 'em. And as for pistols . . . why, rifles are the trick out here . . . and who else has a saddle like this one?"

"And the mare?" she asked.

His mouth twitched. "Poor girl," he said, but instantly made himself smile again, then started for the mark.

The ripple of the news had spread before him like fire through dead grass. Now it roared far away like waves over shallows—among the Blackfeet, who hoped to see the Crow humbled at last; among the whites of the fort, who heard the whisper that the young greenhorn was a fool sure to lose; among the more distant Cheyennes, where a tall chief was moving from group to group and saying two words to each. He was giving them, as he felt, a secret worthy of a price. He was telling each distinguished warrior who he wished to make his friend that, if he would win an easy bet, this was his golden opportunity, by laying money on the white man's horse.

And suddenly the whole focus of attention of all that crowd—men and women, and children with eyes bright as foxes—was gathered once more upon two horses and their riders.

With the Cheyennes determined to bet deep and long, there was plenty of trouble already assured, when Meany, with the best will in the world, made the complications still more serious.

Spotted Calf himself, that noble young chief, found the trader in the crowd and asked him seriously: "You have a knowledge of the horses of your men. Tell me, friend, if the horse of the young man is very fast?"

And Meany answered with a laugh: "You are my friend, Spotted Calf, and now I shall be a friend to you. That young man has just come out here among us, and he is a young fool. He opens his mouth many times, but only a few words come out, and those are for women and children to play with, and not for men to hear. Will a man like that ride a very swift horse?"

Spotted Calf asked no more.

He went away and found his three squaws, and he said to them: "Bring some of my horses. Put robes and beaver pelts on them. Today, I have won a race before the horses left the start. Bring down many horses. If you see my friends, my best friends and companions on the warpath, tell them that the Crow's horse is sure to win."

The squaws left, and the word spread, and the Crows went to their teepees and came staggering down under the weight of their goods.

What man would not bet his very boots on a sure thing?

VI

Young Tarlton jogged his horse around the course. He did not like it; he knew that he was beaten, but he had in his mind to make as good a race as he could. And as he looked down to the gleaming, slender neck of the mare, he bade her good bye in his thoughts.

He had in his heart a single hope, that perhaps she would be able to climb the draw, where the Cheyenne had failed, but when he looked down from the edge above, he saw that the bottom was covered with loose pebbles, and the distance was not sufficient to give a horse a proper run. She could not jump the bank from such a footing, and, if she could not jump it, she certainly could not climb it where the cat-footed Cheyenne stallion had failed.

So he came gloomily back toward the start, and, because he was gloomy, he whistled as clearly as any blackbird that ever flew up from a sunny field of flowers.

Helen Meany, drifting toward him through the press, heard that whistle and understood, and she smiled with tears standing in her eyes.

In the meantime, the excitement among the Indians grew. The Crows by this time were willing to bet their medicine bags on their champion. From the Blackfeet, they could get no wagers, but here came the Cheyennes, keen for plunder.

Of all the warriors who roamed the plains, there were no warriors quite so determined as the Cheyennes. They rode as hard as the Comanches; they charged home with a firmness all their own, and they carried the same thorough-going spirit into all their pursuits. Not even a Sioux was willing to bet with more determined extravagance than the Cheyennes.

They had their tip from their foremost chief. It was almost a duty to take his advice. And besides, they saw before them the sleek beauty of the French mare, and the strange costume of the rider, and the strange saddle in which he rode—all the more reason for having confidence in him.

They came carrying beadwork, blankets, robes

painted and unpainted, knives, guns, decorated pouches, and all the wealth that an Indian prizes, even down to ornamented back rests from their teepees.

They came like a flood among the Crows and the Blackfeet, and wherever warrior met warrior the bets were plighted solemnly. There was no doubt of honest payment, for cheating in such matters was not in the Indian code.

Duncan met Meany in the midst of this babble of bargains.

"The Cheyennes are clean crazy," he said.

"It serves them right," said Meany through his teeth. "With the Cheyennes half bankrupt, we can close and do business with the other two tribes. Little Bull is the one we want out of the way. The brave has advised his people to bet on Tarlton's mare, I hear. And if that's the case, he'll be a chief without a following, in another ten minutes. Look yonder, where the Cheyennes are still boiling up with their stuff. They're gutting their teepees to bet."

In fact, they might have done so, but there was hardly time. For the two riders were now ready, and the two horses were looking each other in the eye at the start.

It was already an important contest. Although surely not one man on the field understood just how great would be the consequences of the ride that young Tarlton was about to give the mare.

But now the starter was in place. The line was freshened and drawn deeper to mark the finish. Spotted Calf himself gave the word and the two were away.

The mare, swift as she was, never had been trained for such work. Her long legs required momentum slowly gained before she could be at her best, and the result was that the Crow darted four lengths into the lead in the very first moment, and the Cheyennes sent up a shrill "Yip! Yip!" of agony.

Once fairly started, however, Camille fairly ate up the shaggy pony and was at his tail when they reached the turf pile at the end of the first stretch. But she floundered heavily in getting about it, while the Crow horse, familiar with the active work of buffalo hunting, trained in exactly this neat maneuver of dodging about the post, whipped around and was off with hardly a single stride lost—off, digging his hoofs into the turf, humping his sturdy back to get again into full speed.

He ran like a hunting dog, rather than like a horse.

The Crows, delirious with pleasure, yelled and chanted and cared not for the ground the mare made up on the back stretch. For though she was close again at the turf pile, gaining all through the wide swing around the draw, still she lost terribly at the turn. Her legs seemed to shoot away beneath her, and she sprawled and staggered.

The horses flew away. The crowd grew suddenly hushed, for many a fine buffalo robe, and many a beaver pelt, many a knife, and many a good rifle lay piled for the betting. One side grew silent lest the surety of their victory should be snatched from them, and the other side grew silent with a final, desperate hope. So the last pile was turned, and they shot off on the back stretch, with the Crow warrior a good six lengths in the lead.

He could not be headed, and he knew it. And he sat straight up, and threw away his club and smote the side of the willing pony with the flat of his hand.

Tarlton saw this as he stretched the mare away for the finish, and he knew that his opponent was right. Nothing but wings could catch him now, along that course around the draw, and no matter how desperately the mare might increase her speed, the distance was far too short. Even now she was hardly gathered into her full stride.

Then the great thought leaped into the mind of Tarlton, and he laughed, fierce and short, as he gathered the reins and leaned above the mare's withers. He drew her in, well to the left of the course, on a straight line for the finish, on a straight line for the point where the draw was the deepest.

And as the Cheyennes saw, they raised a deep-throated wail of misery. Their bets were lost. More than one knife was automatically fingered at that moment.

But Tarlton, driving the mare on, did not slacken her to take the dip into the draw. Instead, he increased her pace as she went at it, and, rising a little, he threw her at the ditch.

Three strides away she saw his purpose and her ears flattened. It looked death to her, no doubt, for she saw the great width of the gap, and the sharp edge of the farther bank, hard, sunbaked, and edged with rocks like the teeth of a shark.

She needed no telling to see that a slip and a fall, or a short leap, would mean a broken back, or a belly ripped open. And she was, moreover, a young and untried mare with none of the confidence of the hunting field behind her. She had only the proud blood that flowed in her veins, and the love of her rider, and her trust in the firm hands that held her, and the strong will that thrust down the reins.

So her ears at the last moment pricked gallantly forward. She rose and hurled herself gallantly upward. The big pebble-strewn bed of the draw gleamed beneath her, the farther bank rose sheer and high—and then she struck.

Right on the edge she landed, but with her hoofs bunched beneath her. The shock slewed Tarlton sideways in the saddle. Then, scrambling fiercely, the mare struggled to the flat beyond.

Before her lay a straight way to the finish; she heard the yells of the revived Cheyennes, the silence of the Crows and the Blackfeet.

"By Jupiter!" cried Duncan.

And Meany, remembering his message to Spotted Calf, gaped, and felt his heart turn cold.

There was still an excellent chance for the Crow rider, however, for though he rode upon a slant, so great was his original lead that he still was closer to the goal. But hardly had the mare got under way than this hope was lost.

She was no dodger about corners, but, in the open, she ran light as a frightened deer. Now could be seen the reason for the long legs of the English thoroughbred. She did not run. She bounded, and with every bound there seemed the thrust and beat of wings buoying her in the air.

The Crow, with face contorted, thrusting his torturing knuckles into the ribs of his pony, saw a velvet streak slide past him, and the sun flashed on the neck and the working shoulders of the mare. By that advantage she won the race.

There had been a long channel beyond the finish, left empty of spectators so that the horses could be pulled up. Right to the end of this the mare labored before she could control the long stroke of her gallop, and then it was as though a sea shut in about her, for every Cheyenne swayed in with outstretched hands, shouting and laughing, and stroking her. And she, hand-raised and gentled as she was, sniffed at them kindly and moved with extreme care lest one of her hoofs should descend with bruising weight upon the moccasined feet.

However, they let her go on, though slowly, giving back a little on either side—the Cheyennes with bright, laughing faces; the Crows stunned; the Blackfeet sullen.

Tarlton went straight on until he came to the place where Helen Meany sat her horse. She took his hand, with a gasp.

How had he done it? How had he thought of such a thing?

"Why," said Tarlton, "the worst gambler has to win once in a while, and I suppose that I'd used up my share of the bad luck before."

"No," she told him, "that was quick thinking . . . and good nerves. I . . . I could almost see your face when you turned toward home and got the idea. And what a beauty!" She touched the wet head of the mare.

He drew her attention away from the mare, and away from himself, embarrassed.

"Look yonder," he said. "It seems to me that your father is in a good deal of trouble."

Just past the outskirts of the crowd, they could see Meany, and before him was Spotted Calf, talking with the air of a very angry man.

VII

Hot as Spotted Calf seemed, he was hotter than his looks. From poor Meany he demanded at once an explanation as to why the trader had passed on to him such wrong information concerning the young white man and his horse.

Meany answered, as many another has answered in the same position: "Spotted Calf, I told you the thing I think. What else can a man say to his best friend?"

"That is true," said Spotted Calf. "But how had the young man proved himself a fool?"

The trader struggled in his mind, and he was about to tell the other that this was a thing that he could not explain to any but a white man with a knowledge of other whites, when he realized that such an answer would be as good as none. And Meany began to perspire copiously. More than a little had been taken from the Blackfeet by the luck of the Cheyennes, but still the treasure trove was in the teepees of the Blackfeet—they had the wealth of beaver pelts. Now, in the hostile air of the chief, he read at once the loss of all chance to trade for a single skin.

No doubt, by the morning, the Blackfeet squaws would strike their tents and away the long column would travel toward the next fort. Not only would that chance of trade be lost, but forever after, unless some difficult stroke were accomplished, the Blackfeet would shun Fort Meany.

"Brother," said the perplexed trader, "this young man is a great gambler."

"It is very well," said Spotted Calf—who was the most ardent gamester in his entire nation—"that a young man should love the warpath more than the gathering of wealth."

"Aye, but what of the dice box?"

"The dice speak the will of Tirawa," said the chief, looking up.

"Very well," said Meany. "This young man never has been on the warpath."

"Is it not true that all the white men, before they come to the Indians and learn the ways of a man, live soft and grow fat?"

Blankly Meany stared upon the angry chief. In his heart, he consigned young Tarlton to a deep and black and fiery pit. "You can see for yourself that he has no brass tacks in the stock of his rifle," he ventured.

"Yes," said the chief, "but he has no rifle."

"What is a man without a gun?" asked Meany. "What would you say in your own tribe?"

"In my tribe," said the chief proudly, "we fill the hands of our brave young men with weapons. A big teepee does not mean a big heart, and painted buffalo robes do not make a strong hand."

Checked at every point, the trader exclaimed:

"Everything about him is foolish! Look at his strange clothes, and his saddle, and the pink of his face!"

Said the Blackfoot: "The Pawnee wolves have cropped heads, but they shoot straight and their heads are wise. May they have bad fortune. Why should a man be judged by the clothes on his back, or the length of his hair?"

"Even his horse is not like the strong and quick-footed horses men use on the prairie for hunting the buffalo," said Meany at last.

"No, no!" exclaimed the chief, his face and eyes suddenly burning. "That is a horse that men would use for hunting men."

"Friend, friend," said Meany, "as a matter of fact, this man does not even know how to shoot a rifle. He uses only a pair of little pistols."

"Does he do that? I believe it," said the chief. "His heart is so big that he laughs at the warriors when they shoot at a distance. He wishes to rush his horse in close and fight hand-to-hand. The fire of his gun burns the body of his enemy. Is that the act of a fool, or of a hero?"

"Brother . . ."—Meany began hopelessly and helplessly, but the chief struck in sharply: "You call me brother and friend many times, but sweet words do not fill the pot."

Without further speech, he threw his robe over his shoulder and was about to go off when Meany determined to make a last effort.

He exclaimed: "My friend, Spotted Calf, my heart is sore because you have become angry with me! I understand why you have turned against me. It is because you have lost many good robes, and you have bet some weapons, some knives and rifles, also. But now I will prove to you that I am something more than a friend in words. Come to my teepee. There you will find long rifles that cannot miss the mark. You will find bullets and powder. You will find the finest knives, and keen hatchets that sink into wood the breadth of your hand. There are bags of colored beads, and there are bags of bright crystal-clear beads. There are spearheads of steel that run through a shield of tough bull-hide like a finger through sand. You shall come up with me, and you shall say what you have lost in the betting. Then take twice as much from my lodge. It shall be yours . . . we shall be brothers!"

This forensic effort left Meany quite winded, and his heart jumped when he saw the chief start with surprise and with delight, but instantly the brow of the Blackfoot darkened again.

"When the sun rose," said Spotted Calf, "my people called me a chief. The young men smiled when I passed them. The old men followed me with their eyes. When I spoke, even the women were silent." He scowled at the trader. "I was given a word by you. I thought it was a true word. I, Spotted Calf, have only one tongue, and it is straight. So I gave them freely the knowledge that you had given to me. I could have bet on the race to fill my own teepee. I would not do that. I wish to make the hearts of the warriors glad. It would be a proper thing, then, that all the others should lose, and that only I should have my losses repaid to me?"

He paused. And, for a brief instant, the trader even contemplated repaying the losses of the entire body of the Blackfeet through that unlucky gambling. But then he saw that the thing was impossible. Their rapacity would instantly strip him of everything. Therefore, he had to remain silent, while the chief went on.

"I have walked on many warpaths. I have led many war parties. We have ridden out on our own horses, and we have ridden home on the horses of the enemy. But now when I pass, men will turn their heads and look the other way. Voices will mutter behind me. All the work of my life is made nothing today."

He gathered his robe suddenly about him and strode away without uttering another word.

Meany gloomily looked after him, bitterly cursing the day that he ever had laid eyes upon him. And, at that moment, he saw Duncan riding toward him, with an expression by no means pleasant.

They met each other, scowling.

The trader had no chance to speak before

Duncan exclaimed: "The devil is loose on all sides! The Crows are boiling. They blame me because I suggested that they match their man against young Tarlton. Who could have guessed that he would take such a chance? But no . . . it's exactly the chance that a fool would take and a sensible man wouldn't dream of."

"Are the Crows very hot?" asked Meany darkly.

"Hot? They're boiling. That fellow who rode the horse is Rising Bird. I didn't know he was a chief, but it seems that he is, and he swears that I have tricked him. All the Crows are furious. They say that we've trimmed them, and the luck is up. Rising Bird says that he is going to pack his goods and leave in the morning, and the rest of the Crows will undoubtedly follow them."

"Of course they will," said Meany. Then he added: "The Blackfeet are going, too."

"That leaves the Cheyennes," said Duncan, and sighed. "And the market is already almost crowded with buffalo robes. Beaver, beaver, is the thing we must have."

Meany said: "Duncan, who told you that this man was an idiot?"

"Who, Tarlton?"

"Aye, Tarlton."

"You could see for yourself."

Meany was not above quoting. "You can't tell a man by the length of his hair, or the cut of his coat," he declared.

"Hello!" exclaimed Duncan. "And that's it, is it? You've turned your teeth on me, Meany?"

"You've ruined the fort before it had a chance to do business," said Meany bitterly. "I've put the work of my life into the building of that fort, and you've torn it down for me with this day's work!"

"Then build it again or let it rot," said Duncan. "I've done with a man who cries when his fingers are burned in a fire that he helped to make. Who sneered the loudest at Tarlton, I ask you? But I see now that he's the sort of a man that you want out here. Your daughter seems to have the same idea."

And he turned his horse and rode off.

Meany looked after him with an increasing despair. No matter how he felt about the situation, he saw that he should have been silent about his troubles before the trader. There was no more experienced man among all those who dealt with Indians than was Duncan. There was no man whose word went so far with other traders. And now there was no doubt but that he would turn his back on the fort and that the other traders would be apt to follow him away. In that case, Fort Meany, indeed, would be the grave of the Meany fortune.

Then he looked with a wild eye across the crowd, and it happened that he saw at that moment his daughter Helen riding beside young Tarlton, and the two laughing gaily together.

Meany ran suddenly and breathlessly up to them. "Get to the fort!" he shouted at his daughter. "Your gadding about in the crowd is making a fool of me. Get to the fort, and stay in your room till I come there!"

And then he brushed past the astonished pair and went off through the crowd, bitterly noting the triumphant Cheyennes, their arms loaded down with the plunder of the betting.

VIII

When that paternal bomb had been exploded before Helen Meany, she looked about her with a startled air, but Tarlton nodded reassuringly.

"It's nothing you've done except being with me," he said. "It's my luck. If I don't get into trouble myself, I get my friends there."

"But what can *you* have done?" asked the girl.

"The way I work it out," he said, "there's only one answer that's right, and there's a thousand that are wrong. So I'm not surprised when I'm wrong. I don't know how I've added up here, unless your father was betting on the Crow horse."

"Ah, he's not so small as to keep malice for that," Helen insisted. "I must go on to the fort. How angry he was. I suppose . . . I suppose . . . ," she faltered.

And Tarlton, going on beside her, looked her steadily in the eyes, as he had looked at more than one girl before her in his reckless life.

"Suppose I want to have even a glimpse of you again . . . unless I'm sent out of the fort?" he said.

She hesitated, and flushed. "My room is in the southwest corner . . . the second story of the log cabin there. I . . ." Her flush suddenly grew hotter. She nodded to him jerkily, and rode off, as though ashamed of what she had said.

Young Tarlton looked after her with a good deal of satisfaction, and even with a faint smile on his lips that had in it as much contemptuous amusement as admiration. Then a hand twitched his stirrup, and he looked down into the ugly, full-lipped face of the half-breed Blackfoot who had served him as a teamster on the way across the prairie.

This rascal had a face like a stupid mask, except that now and again his little eyes glinted like the eyes of a pig. They glinted now, as he said in good English, for he had been long among the whites—for a certain time in prison: "Little Bull wants to see you."

"And who is Little Bull?" asked Tarlton. "What kind of a bull may he be, Young River?"

Young River grinned vastly. "Little Bull is the Cheyenne chief," he said. "There are others. He is the big chief, the war chief. Just now his heart is very warm. He wants to talk to you."

"Friend?"

"Friend," said Young River, and he translated the term into the only meaning that he could understand. "Friend good enough to give you teepee and squaw and horses and rifle. Very big friend to you now."

"Ah, he bet on the mare?"

"He bet. He make all the other Cheyennes bet. That was Little Bull. You better go talk."

Tarlton, willing enough, followed his guide through the green meadows where the crowd was beginning to break up, forming in little groups, here and there, to talk over the events of the day. Those who remained were chiefly the losing Blackfeet and the Crows. As for the Cheyennes, they had made off with their loot to their teepees. Those who had not, looked after Tarlton with no very friendly eyes.

At this moment a raw-boned trader, dressed more like an Indian than a white man, and mounted on a long-maned Indian pony, into whose hair shells and beads were braided, called to Tarlton and pointed to the side.

"There comes your man to talk turkey," he said.

Tarlton, turning, saw that the defeated champion was coming slowly toward him. He rode a fine pony and led behind him the strange-looking beast that had run so brilliantly that day. The face of this Crow warrior was as blankly indifferent to those around him as though its features had been cut of stone. On the back of the pony appeared the rifle, and all the other accouterments of which the bet consisted.

Tarlton checked his horse, and the trader turned in his pony to see the payment of the debt. Instantly a curious little group was formed.

Said the trader, as the Crow wound his way among the groups of people: "Here's the only touch of luck that I've had since I left Saint Louis, this trip. I liked the look of your horse, stranger, and I got down a couple of bets on her. This pony is one of 'em. This robe is another." He lifted a beautiful painted robe from behind the cantle of his saddle. "One day a month like this would keep me pretty. You've brought me that luck, stranger. Tarlton is your name, I hear, and they call me Sam Quigley."

Tarlton shook the hard, lean hand.

"When I come out from Saint Louis," said Quigley, grown talkative, "I left my luck behind me. Agent died, and his son made up my packs . . . not the way I'd ordered 'em, but the way he thought they'd oughta be. Sent out a lot of canvas. Now, why in heaven's name canvas for plains Indians, I ask? Sent me toys, too, that kids might like, but that even an Indian can see ain't worth a trick. Sent me a box of phosphorus. Why phosphorus? What trick can I do with that stuff? Sent me some fancy shotguns, too. They don't shoot ducks, they shoot buffalo, out here . . . and some of them buffalo they hunt has only got two legs, and I half wish that fool of an agent was one of the herd."

This outburst came in a quiet, careless drawl. There was much heat in the words, but none whatever in the voice that pronounced them, and the big man looked almost sleepy as he concluded.

In the meantime, up came the Crow champion, and held out the lead rope of rawhide to Tarlton. He said: "Sometimes a long jump will win a race, friend, and it is a good trick. It gets many horses."

He was about to turn away, when Tarlton called after him. "Friend," said the boy, looking uncertainly at the horse, "what a man cannot eat, he ought not to kill."

"That is true," said the Crow gloomily, gathering his brows as he waited and wondered at what might come.

"These long rifles," said Tarlton, "I never have learned to use. I already have a powder horn and a pouch for bullets. Your saddle, you see, is not what I am used to riding on. Why should I take things that I cannot use? And as for the horse, it would be wrong for me to take a good horse from a famous chief and warrior who knows so well how to ride him. It was not the horse or the rider that was beaten, but luck and a trick sometimes will win, my friend."

Downright embarrassment in not knowing what to do with this winning had really dictated the answer that Tarlton made, and the Crow looked at him in bewilderment. His lips parted to make a sharp answer, such as his pride dictated to him. For he had come more prepared for battle than for friendship, and the heart of the Crow was burning in him when he remembered all the triumphs that his pony had won among his own people, and over the fastest horses of the plains.

Here, in a single stroke, his fortune was restored to him. He stared at Tarlton, and then he was able to see—for an Indian is as acutely sensitive as a child—that there was no scorn or contempt in the face of the white man.

Then the eyes of Rising Bird widened a little. He grunted something in his Crow tongue that Tarlton did not understand, but he knew, as most Indians did by this time, that the white man's greeting was a grip of the hands. So he stretched out his own. Like a vise of iron those powerful fingers closed over the hand of Tarlton. But he who has held straining hunters balanced across weary miles of hunting fields has a grip second to none, and the grip of the white man steadily met that crushing pressure.

Pleasure and surprise gleamed in the eyes of the sturdy warrior. He grunted again, and, turning without another word, he took his way back among the people. They stared after him, amazed that he should depart with the articles of the wager.

"What did he say?" asked Tarlton. "I didn't understand that last *woof-woof.*"

"I know the Crow lingo," said long Sam Quigley. "He means that his teepee is your teepee and his horses are all your horses because Rising Bird is a friend."

Tarlton went on with Young River, and the half-breed eyed his companion with the keenest attention.

"What trade you make out of that?" he asked.

"What trade do you mean?" said Tarlton.

"Where any profit?" asked Young River.

"Oh, out of that?" said Tarlton. He squinted at the sky. "I'll tell you what, Young River," he said. "I like to gamble as well as the next fellow, but I don't like to collect by a trick."

"Trick?" questioned Young River. "Wouldn't Rising Bird jump his pony across the ditch if he could?"

"He never would have raced that course if he'd known that the ditch could be jumped," said Tarlton. "As a matter of fact, what I did was to win the race by running inside of the flags that were set up to mark the course, and really it was hard luck for that fellow that I should get the money. Besides, he rode hard, and he rode well, and he should have had the pleasure of beating three horses instead of two."

Young River looked at him, for the moment, not as a hard-headed Indian, but as a wondering Negro. For, from time to time, one never could tell which part of his mixed blood would come the nearest to the surface. But at last he said: "I not understand."

"Why not?"

"You come here to make money?"

"Yes."

"Then you play dice on the way and lose three parts in four. You pay. You not say no. Now come better luck. You win. You give back everything. You tell Young River why?"

Tarlton looked down into the wondering, puzzled face of the half-breed and shook his head. "You wouldn't understand," he said.

"We got plenty time," said Young River.

"Oh, no," said Tarlton. "It would take twenty or thirty generations to make you see the point."

IX

They came to the river's edge and found a considerable sprinkling of people up and down the watercourse. Topping the highest slope was the Blackfoot encampment, which covered much more ground than those of the two other tribes. To the left lay the Crows. To the right were the Cheyennes, and toward the tall teepees of that tribe the half-breed was now leading the way.

Meany was seen to the left, having an ardent discussion with two chiefs of the Blackfeet. He even had crossed the river.

Sam Quigley pointed out: "That's a fool move for an old head like Meany. He oughta know better than that, now that the Piegans are worked up about that horse race."

He turned his newly won pony, and straightway pushed across the stream to give his support to the owner of the fort.

Young River said: "Pretty easy to see where other man is fool . . . also pretty easy step in same place." And he jerked his thumb toward Quigley as the latter rode off.

"You mean to say that the Piegans might tackle those two men?" asked Tarlton.

"Why not?" Young River said with a shrug of his broad shoulders. "Two men, many coups, two scalps. Why not? There is always room on the coup stick to count more deeds."

"I think that you'd like a few white scalps yourself," said Tarlton.

"No, no," answered the half-breed. "I like to eat every day in the year. So I stay white."

Young River never placed his ideas upon a lofty basis; he was a pure materialist—so pure a materialist that the ideal rarely entered his mind at all.

"Does it look fair to you," asked Tarlton, who

loved to draw out the brute mind of Young River, "that two men should be jumped by a whole crowd? If there's any danger of that, I'll ride over and give them a hand."

"No, no," repeated Young River. "You make more trouble by going. Nobody see one man . . . maybe see two . . . whole people see three."

This seemed logical. The Blackfeet would have even less hesitation in attacking three men than they would in tackling one or two. There would be so much more to gain by striking the first blow, if there was any sort of trouble.

"They're honorable people," persisted Tarlton to himself. "They won't hit out at helpless men."

"One coup is one coup," persisted this businessman of the plains.

"Where is the honor," asked Tarlton, "if a coup is counted? It's in the danger that a man has faced that he gets honor, eh?"

Young River smiled and shook his head. "You look buffalo wolf."

"Well?"

"Is he wise?"

"I suppose he is."

"Does he charge at grizzly?"

"Naturally not."

"If he find buffalo calf lying down in the grass, does wolf call big bull buffalo, asleep in the sun? No, he eats calf pretty quick."

"Well, what of that?"

"Wolf very wise," said Young River.

"You mean that men ought to act like that, too, and only kill where there's no chance of resistance?"

"One coup is one coup," insisted the half-breed Piegan.

"Well," said Carlton, "we look at the same thing from different sides of the fence."

"Not understand," Young River said deliberately.

"Of course you don't, and it would take a million years to make you."

"One coup is one coup," said the Indian. "The man of fire, even, came down to count his coup."

"What was that?" asked Tarlton.

"You saw Spotted Calf?"

"The Blackfoot chief? Yes."

"His father, his father, his father, his father," said Young River.

"His great-great-grandfather, you mean?"

"Well, he was a great chief, too. He was called Spotted Calf, also. That is why the Piegans call this one Young Spotted Calf. Because they still remember that other Spotted Calf because of what happened to him."

"And what happened to him?"

"He was a great chief. He had killed many enemies. The Cheyennes knew him, and his lodge was filled with the scalps of the Pawnee wolves. So it came that this Spotted Calf began

72

to think that he had only to call, and the Sky People would hear him and come down from the blue and give him help."

"He was betting on his run of luck, then," said Tarlton. "And that's all right, if a man doesn't keep doubling the stakes."

"I not understand," Young River said with a touch of impatience.

"You ought to," said Tarlton, "because it's a thing that you never do. But go on."

"Spotted Calf took a great war party and he rode with them over the hills. He found the Crows sleeping in their camp. He rode in among them. It was a dark night. In the sky a man of fire appeared riding a horse of fire. He plunged from cloud to cloud. The Crows saw him and they were afraid. They saw him reaching out his bright lance of fire. They turned and ran, and the Blackfeet rode in under Spotted Calf and counted coups, many and many, and they tore off scalps until their arms were very weary.

"Then they went among the teepees and they took all that they wished. They took some young children to raise as Blackfeet and teach them to take Crow scalps, which is a very good thing. Then they rode away through the rain. They came far off in the hills and they made a camp where there were trees. The rain was very loud on the branches."

He paused a moment, and Tarlton felt that he

could hear the crash of the volleyed rain upon the trees.

"Then the man and the horse of white fire were seen again in the clouds of the sky. But they did not stay there. Suddenly they jumped out of the sky and rushed down. They saw the rider stretch out his spear. There was a great shout that came from a greater voice than any warrior's, as the rider from the sky counted coup.

"All the Piegans tried to cover their eyes, but they could not help seeing a blast of white fire as the rider of the horse of fire sprang up into the clouds again. After a long time the oldest and the bravest of the warriors were not afraid to come to see what had happened. They found that the horse of Spotted Calf was dead. Spotted Calf himself was burned to ashes, and crumbled when they touched him, and from the tree under which he was camped every leaf was burned.

"These things were told to my father by old men among the Piegans, and, therefore, I know them to be true. Also, men can tell what caused the thing, because everyone in the tribe knew that Spotted Calf thought he was as good as any one of the Sky People. He talked of them as though they were his brothers. That was what made them angry."

"Why didn't they let the Crows kill him then?" asked Tarlton.

"Because," said the half-breed, "Spotted Calf was very brave, and because he was very cunning. He made his plans so very well that the Sky People themselves were interested, and they said to the man of fire . . . 'Wait. Let us see what this Piegan will do tonight.' Then, when they had seen how cleverly he did everything, and how many scalps his people took, they laughed and rubbed their noses, because it is true that the Sky People love the Blackfeet."

"Humph!" said Tarlton. "And then they rubbed out Spotted Calf after admiring his methods so much?"

"They wanted to punish him, but they also wanted to show that they admired him. They could have sent another warrior to kill him, of course. But they would not do that."

"They sent down a lightning bolt to kill him, instead?"

"Lightning?" said Young River.

"Well, of course. That was what killed him. A blast of lightning happened to jump out of the sky and hit the poor fellow."

"Ah?" Young River mused. "And what about the horse of fire?"

"Lightning playing in the clouds, of course," said the white man.

"In the form of a white horse of fire?"

"This happened a long time ago," said Tarlton, "and you know that people can't get things straight, even if they repeat them only the next day."

"Perhaps that may be true . . . among the white men. But I am speaking about my own people, who I know, and every Piegan can tell the truth exactly."

"Are you a Piegan?" said Tarlton.

"Yes," Young River answered with a rare touch of pride.

"Ah, well," said Tarlton, "I won't argue. But I thought that you had a sense of humor, Young River."

"Not understand," Young River said.

"Why, of course you don't," said Tarlton, "because then the laugh would be on you."

Young River looked at him a little wistfully. There were times when he felt that he was actually inside the mind of the white man, but then again a wall arose between them, as at this moment. He even sighed a little, but, the next instant, his mind was given entirely to the problem before him, and that was the practical amount of benefit that his master—for the moment Tarlton stood in that relation to him—could gain from his interview with the Cheyenne chief. They had now come down the riverbank to the proper point, and on the farther side they could see Little Bull himself.

X

"And now," Tarlton said to Young River, "if there is danger to Meany back there from the Blackfeet, why isn't there danger to you and me, here, from the Cheyennes? Or are they better people?"

"The Piegans," said Young River, "are the best people in the world."

"By that," Tarlton said, "you mean the readiest people to lift a scalp or count a coup, and the handiest at stabbing a man in the back?"

Young River was clever enough to see that his own logic now was being used against him, and he winced a little, and then a gleam of amusement came into his small eyes.

"The man of the fort," he said, "has made enemies of the Piegans by telling them to bet against your horse."

"Why should he do that?"

"Because he is not a wise man. If he had waited longer, he would have known you better."

"Well, but today he wanted to know my horse, and not me."

"That is not true. Horses fall down, but men win races. And there is Little Bull to thank you for winning many bets for him."

So Tarlton crossed the river at the side of his

77

ugly guide, and he found a rich welcome from the Cheyennes on the farther shore.

There were several things about Tarlton that delighted them—his youth, his fine presence, his open face, and, above all, the horse that he rode. For that leap of his horse had already become an established legend in the minds of the old men who had seen it. In a single year it would take on the dimensions of a fable, and everything would be multiplied by ten, from the length of the leap to the height of the wall of the draw, and, above all, the value of the bets they had won from the unlucky Crows and Blackfeet.

However, those bets were really considerable.

The teepee of Little Bull stood close to the river, and in front of it were the bets that he had captured owing to the race. He had at least three rifles and half a dozen painted robes, to begin with. Half a dozen horses were held at one side. There were a few beaded suits, a number of pairs of moccasins, and a great display of cutlery, since cold steel was the particular passion of the chief's heart. There were hatchets, axes, many knives—from butcher knives to plain hunting knives—spearheads, and everything down to the metal mountings of a bridle that had happened to catch his fancy.

When Tarlton was aware of these things, he guessed the purpose for which he had been brought. And he flushed a little, for he saw what he would be urged to do, and he did not like the role.

Little Bull came out to meet him, and greeted him with a clumsy, formal handshake. Then he sat Tarlton down, while about them appeared at least a score of dignified warriors. They were not invited to attend the conversation, but they were not driven away, and therefore their curiosity was satisfied. They laid their hands upon the mare, upon the saddle, upon the naked, iron stirrups, the short leathers, the open, very light saddle. They touched the ends of the bit and made out that it was a simple snaffle. Everything that they saw, they admired with a soft chorus of grunts. Small boys, naked and brown-red, pressed behind them, around them, between their legs, to peer at the beautiful horse.

But in spite of this press of people, there was a soft decorum in the voices. No Indian people of the plains possessed the majestic dignity of the Cheyennes, just as none possessed such a Roman steadiness in battle.

In the meantime, the chief had produced his pipe, filled and lighted it, and Tarlton, with grave care—instructed a little from a distance by the half-breed—managed to accept it in the proper fashion.

The speech of Little Bull was quietly to the point. He said that he had not been a rich man before this day, and that after this day there still would be many richer men than he in the tribe. However, he had found a great windfall,

"Because," he said, "as I passed the rider of the mare, I heard him speak, and I distinctly heard him say that she would surely win if he cared to have her."

This was duly translated by Young River, that nine-tongued interpreter. And Tarlton blinked, for he remembered his jesting remark that had been so seriously interpreted.

"Say to me, therefore," said the chief, "what you will take to remember Little Bull, and that he is a friend and not ungrateful to those who do good for him. Look at this heap that I have won. I know that the white man wishes to have beaver skins. There is that heap, there. And the white man wishes to have rifles . . . and, see, there are some. You and your friend must go among these things. Where there are four, take two. Where there are three, take two, also. Because a good division of these things will be the division that makes my friend happy."

"Tell him," said Tarlton to the half-breed, "that I cannot take anything that I have not bought."

Young River made a gesture of bewilderment. "Here is enough," he said, "to buy twenty horses, at least, besides those horses, yonder."

"Very well," said Tarlton, "let the twenty horses remain."

"Ah," said the half-breed, "if you will say this,

remember that everyone is not as rich as you are, brother, and everyone does not have such beautiful mares that run so swiftly, or little pistols that shoot so straight. There is I, brother. Remember me. Take what the large heart of the chief offers to you, and I shall be able to take from you everything else that you do not need."

At this speech, Tarlton shook his head and swallowed a smile. Therefore, with almost a groan, the half-breed translated the last speech of his master exactly as it had been made. It caused a good deal of astonishment among the Cheyennes. The fine mare ceased to be an object of attention, at once. An old woman was seen to bend over her son, to point and to whisper: "Yonder sat a man who refused a gift of twenty horses."

The chief, in the meantime, was in dismay and in some doubt. He even frowned, as though he felt that there was an insult hidden somewhere in this remark, or a challenge.

Then Tarlton said: "Explain this, Young River. Tell him that I am glad the running of the mare and her good jumping made him better off. But, after all, the best thing that he can offer me is friendship. You understand, Young River. Put it in his own words, and in your own way. Don't try to turn the English words into Cheyenne, until you feel that you know what I mean. The fact is, that I could not take any of these things. They would be payment. I'm not to be paid, after all, but the mare. And how can anyone pay her?"

Young River sighed. He saw a handsome profit lost to his master; he saw, also, a chance for a handsome gain lost to himself, for he knew that the fingers of Tarlton were wide set, and that much flowed through them. However, he saw, too, the chance to make his speech, and he made it. There is nothing that an Indian loves better. And here was the opportunity of a lifetime, in the sense of a red man. For a young man, a Piegan, was able to stand before the great Cheyennes, and speak to the wise men and the chiefs in their own tongue, and hold them spellbound.

The Indian is generous, but he is as apt at taking as he is at giving. The philosophy of the white man, however, even if it could not be exactly understood and imitated, appeared a noble thing. Like children, the Cheyennes smiled. They looked upon one another, greatly pleased and astonished. They looked upon Tarlton and nodded. Certainly his idea was most acceptable to the red men.

Only Little Bull was troubled. He said, when the speech was ended: "These are very good words. But now I am like snow on the mountains. The sun begins to shine. I melt, and there is no place to flow. Well, brother, if there is only friendship to be given, let there be much of that. We do not forget, if you will remember. I speak a little for myself, but also for many of the

Cheyennes. I spoke to them. When I heard your voice speak, I knew that what you said was true, because I could see that you were wise. I spoke to the famous warriors. They heard me. They took their horses and loaded them with goods. They went down and they made their bets against the Crows and the Blackfeet, who are not so rich, tonight."

He got up, and, taking from his shoulders the fine robe that was gathered about him, he drew it around Tarlton.

"In this manner," said Little Bull, "we remember one another. There is no teepee among the Cheyennes that is not open to you. There is no sun too hot for us to give you shade, and there is no winter wind so cold that it can reach you when you do come to us."

He would have made a longer speech, but there was a sudden shouting down the river, far away from them, and then the ringing explosion of rifles.

Voices were raised among the outer ring of the Cheyennes, and Young River leaped to Tarlton and cried in his ear: "Now is the time to forget fine talk and pretty words. They are murdering the white men before the camp of the Piegans. Ride back to the fort! Ride back to the fort! Who can tell when the Cheyennes will forget the talk they have just been making and will be glad to take scalps and count coups instead?"

Tarlton raised his hand to Little Bull, and, turning from him, he leaped into the saddle on the mare. She, nervous instantly with the excitement of her master, swung about and leaped down the riverbank.

Then he could see, straight before him, but at a distance of a furlong at least, a swirl of figures, and the smoke of rifles. The Piegans were sweeping toward the trader and half a dozen other white men who had gathered on the bank about Meany.

Young River did not hesitate. He turned his pony and dashed it through the river and hastened on toward the fort, yelling at his master to follow with all speed, and never turning until he was almost at the fort entrance. When he turned, he saw that Tarlton, instead of heeding the advice of the half-breed, had ridden straight down the green bank of the river and now was among the fighters before the camp of the Piegans.

At the same moment, Young River could see Meany go down, while the tall form of Sam Quigley threw up its arms and fell from the saddle.

XI

It was not altogether a chivalrous instinct that sent Tarlton forward, but very largely the desire of any young man to be present where excitement was gathering. But also there was a vague spur working in him that might be called conscience.

The young mare galloped like the wind, and as she went, devouring the yards with long, bounding strides, Tarlton saw distinctly what was taking place.

While Meany had continued his discussion with the two chiefs, apparently the bad feeling among the Piegans had reached a climax as man after man returned from the horse races and climbed the slope to the camp, many of them on foot—for the good reason that their horses had been lost. Some were carrying their saddles and rawhide lariats, and others were empty-handed. There were some who had gambled away the very clothes on their back, and now strode along in loin straps alone.

Meany, whatever his eloquence, had not been able to prevent the chiefs from leaving him in disgust; they had ridden up the slope toward the verge of their camp, and they were almost at it when the turmoil began.

Those men of force and dignity had been able

to keep the anger of the younger men in check, but as soon as they were gone, the youths turned upon Meany as the author of their losses. They had poured in upon him, and the white men around him, and a brisk struggle began. Rifles were discharged, but the range was very close, and there was little mischief at first.

It was simply a turmoil of tumbling bodies, and the strength and the united valor of the whites kept the red men at bay.

But that could not last long. As Tarlton swept up on the mare, he saw four of the men from the fort dive from the bank into the river. At the same time Meany, attempting to swing his horse about, was overtaken by a hundred hands and instantly mastered, while Quigley was shot from his horse.

Tarlton could tell that it was impossible for him to do the slightest good to Meany, for the press of the Piegans was too thick about him. He doubted for the safety of his own skin, but he could not help trying to save Quigley.

That big man lay prone on the grass, then gradually pried himself up on one elbow, stunned, but instinctively struggling. And, luckily, he was on the verge of the riverbank, the water swishing not two yards from where he had fallen from his horse in his retreat. The Piegan who had fired the shot, throwing aside his rifle, rushed in, tugging out his knife as he did so.

Tarlton's pistol was in his hand by this time,

and the shot was easy. But in all his life of gaming and dueling, he never had fired at the back of a human being, and he could not begin now. Instead, he brought the barrel of the gun down on the head of the Blackfoot. The latter was more startled than hurt. He was not even stunned, but, in the shock of horror at this unexpected attack from the rear, he let the knife fall from his hand and actually threw himself headlong into the river.

It was that which saved the life of Tarlton, and the life of Quigley as well—that and the intervention of the chiefs, who now had returned from higher up the slope. They shouted, and the young men heard them. Besides, they were weak with laughter at the ridiculous sight of the warrior who had been frightened into the water. Tarlton drew up, helped Quigley onto the saddle before him, and then crossed the river and jogged without haste up the farther slope to the fort.

He was still dizzy. He felt as does a man who is about to be sucked into the heart of a whirlpool, and then is suddenly cast up to the calm surface, free from danger. So it was with him, and luck had stood at his side. If he had felled the Piegan, he now saw, a dozen sure rifles would have blown him from the saddle. But the battle had suddenly turned into a jest, and he went free.

However, looking back, he saw the crowd still thick, whirling around a knotted center, as the

Piegans carried poor Meany up to their camp, and the heart of Tarlton suddenly sickened within him.

Quigley was perfectly composed.

"I've lost a mighty smart young pony," he said to Tarlton, "with a fine lot of beads wove into him, too. One look at that horse would've got me the finest squaw that ever beaded moccasins among the Crows, and that's the nation I'm gonna marry into. However, it's a mighty sight better to have shank's pony, than no horse at all, and I'd be red-headed by this time, if you hadn't come boomin' up when you did, young man."

In this leisurely fashion he thanked Tarlton as the two came to the fort.

In the meantime, the alarm had gone out from Fort Meany, and, with the crack of the first rifle, there had been an instant rush toward the fort on the part of the white men, and an instant rush of the Indians away from it. It was almost as though an explosion had happened in the fort, and the fleeing Indians were like the streaks of smoke, blown raggedly outward from the center.

In the fort, there was an instant rallying, and the oldest heads in command sent a strong line to hold the top of the earth wall behind the stout palisade, while others thrust out from the entrance and prepared to meet any drive of the Indians before it could reach to the wagons, which were yet not in full readiness to hold off an assault.

There was ample need for these precautions.

The whole of the three Indian camps had been thrown into turmoil. Living in constant readiness to leap into the saddle, the youngsters of the Piegans were the first out, for they were the tribe that felt the grievance most keenly. The Crows were not far behind them, and the Cheyennes followed from the irresistible force of example.

The latter were by no means friendly toward the Crows and the Blackfeet. But far more than they disliked the other Indians, they hated the whites with a natural and profound hatred. That hate was a fire, and this event had been a sufficient breath of air to make the flames leap.

Now, around and around the plain, at the foot of the slope on which the fort stood, the youngsters coursed their horses. More than half were without saddles, having flung themselves on the first ponies at hand. With the wildest yells, they circled the fort. Most of them carried bows and arrows only. For the older braves, who were the better armed, had not as yet come out to enter the lists; they waited some authoritative word from the chiefs. However, the young vanguard was ready for action, and as they coursed wildly around the fort, had there been the slightest sign of lack of preparedness on the part of the defenders, they would have poured into the gap instantly.

That was the state of affairs that was beginning when Tarlton rode up the slope, with Quigley before him, bleeding rapidly from a wound in the right side that made him pant a little in his drawling speech.

At the head of the party that pushed out from the entrance of Fort Meany was William Duncan, as a matter of course. He had been the first to perceive the necessity, and he was also the first to spring into the position of command. Behind him the best men of the fort were marching, their rifles ready. Other men were climbing the walls of the fort, and others were racing out to throw themselves into the wagon circles, while the nearest wagons were being dragged within the gates of the fort by hand power.

Duncan called out, as Tarlton came up to him: "You've been at it again, have you? I've a mind to have you roped hand and foot and thrown into the river! You've raised a fire again, have you?"

Before Tarlton could answer, Quigley responded for him: "Him that started the trouble was him that sent the Crow to race against Tarlton's mare, Duncan, and him that told the Blackfeet that the bet would be easy ag'in' the mare. I dunno who sent that word, but it never was Tarlton. Maybe you know better than me. Tarlton, here, has just snaked me away from the stake, as you might say. Go on, son. There ain't gonna be any roping of you and throwing of you in rivers, not if there was ten Duncans to ask for it."

Duncan, as part of this speech touched him very closely, drew back with a growl, and Tarlton passed inside the fort.

Of that crowd that stirred within, the first face he saw was that of Helen Meany. White and strained, she passed him. Only for a moment she paused as she ran, and turned toward him. "You let him stay in their hands! You left *him* to the fire!" she cried to Tarlton, and whipped away.

Tarlton's head jerked up as though a bullet had struck him with a heavy impact at that moment.

With his perfect calm, Quigley said: "Now, that's the woman of it, son. It ain't enough that you've caught one fish out of the creek when the family's starvin'. But the only one that'll do the wife is the speckled feller with the funny shape to his head. Oh, I know women. I got a wife and three daughters back at home. That's why I want a Crow squaw, and a peaceful lodge."

The storekeeper, coming out with rifle in hand, paused and helped Quigley down from the back of the mare. Then, they carried him into the fort and stretched him on a cot, with a roll of blankets by way of a pillow under his head.

They opened his shirt, and it could be seen at once that his wound was not very serious. The bullet had raked along the ribs. The blood had flowed until he was appreciably weakened, but when they had washed and bandaged the wound tightly, and given him a strong shot of whiskey, he asked immediately for a pipe.

"Go out and take a look at the trouble," he said to the storekeeper. "You stay here," he added to Tarlton, and the young man unwillingly remained.

"Because there ain't going to be any real trouble now," Quigley explained to his rescuer. "If I thought that there was, this little scratch that I got wouldn't keep me from getting out there with the rest of the men, young feller. But nothing will happen till night."

"And then?" asked Tarlton.

"And then it depends all on Meany. If the Blackfeet murder him and take his scalp, then the whole three tribes will come at us. And, mind you, though they won't rush a place like this in the day, in the night they might jump their horses over this here palisade and rub us all out in no time at all."

XII

In a few minutes, the trouble grew serious. Guns popped far off; they were answered by the single crack of a rifle from the fort.

"Hello!" said Quigley. "The boys are trying to

talk like men, I hear. Go have a look and let me know what's happening."

Tarlton hurried out, and from the top of the embankment, which was lined with men who were digging themselves into shallow rifle pits, he looked out on the green plains and found them fairly awash with riders. At that moment a long line of Cheyennes rushed at the fort, looking like a wave that was sure to overtop the wall. One excited youngster on the embankment discharged a rifle whose bullet went wild, and the Cheyennes, with a yell of triumphant mockery, split to one side and the other and foamed around the walls, shaking spears and guns above their heads.

Tarlton, staring amazedly at this wild scene, was caught from the side and rudely jerked upon his face by a deerskin-clad frontiersman who snarled at him: "If an arrow will go through a buffalo, is your hide tough enough to turn its point, young man?"

The Cheyenne charge was not the last. The Crows poured forward in a flood, and this time half a dozen arrows were loosed by yelling young braves. An arrow struck the bank not two feet from the head of Tarlton and buried itself almost to the feathers, and as the charge washed by, the young man laid hold on the arrow and had to tug twice before it came free. The frontiersman who had dragged him down now looked at him with a nod and a grin.

"You'll learn," he said, "but it comes slow to greenhorns."

Tarlton started back to tell Quigley what he had seen, and on the way he met Helen Meany, carrying two long rifles over the bend of her left arm. She went by him as though he were a bit of blowing mist. Tarlton followed her and touched her shoulder.

"Are you blaming me?" he asked. She turned on him with flaming eyes.

"How can you speak to me?" she cried at him. "How can you hold up your head when real men are around you?"

Tarlton went on to Quigley and told him, quietly, what he had seen from the walls, and the trader twisted this way and that. Then he swore softly.

"It looks almighty black," he admitted. "They're apt to whoop it up all day long, and at the close of the day they'll be boiling for a fight. What will keep them from swarming on board us, like a lot of ants, when the dark comes?"

"Couldn't we light fires outside the palisade?" asked Tarlton.

"And give them good light to shoot us by?"

Tarlton was silent, and Quigley thoughtfully rubbed his head.

"My hair has been mighty loose more times than one," said Quigley. "But I dunno if it ever felt quite so much like fallin' off my head as it does now."

Tarlton rose stiffly from his chair. He said: "I've read a bit in books about white men and Indians. And I've always heard that a dozen steady white men could split the charge of a thousand Indians."

"Aye, you've read of it in books," said Quigley with a sneer. "They write a mighty lot of books about slaughterin' Indians. But if the figgers was added up on the frontier, who would there be the most dead of? Indians or whites? Ask any man on the frontier, and he'll tell you. And how long would this place last without water? And the last I heard, the water tanks wasn't finished."

"No water here?" cried Tarlton. "But then the river is so near?"

"That there river is so dog-gone' far away," said Quigley, "that the gent that tried to get to it would be turned into a porcupine, he'd be stuck so full of arrows, before he ever got to it. Aye, there'd be so many feathers on him that he'd blow away in the wind."

"Well, then," said Tarlton, "a good determined stand, all together, and a sally out . . . ."

"With women and children, and lumberin' wagons, and no chance to hunt meat, and every step we took dogged by a flock of those redskins? It would be a pretty march."

Tarlton looked blankly at him. "Is it as bad as that?" he asked.

"I don't say that we're all scalped yet," said Quigley, "but, if you was to pick out the three orneriest fightin' tribes in the country, you couldn't've picked 'em more exact than the Crows, the Piegans, and those Cheyennes. I'd rather fight any white man than a Cheyenne. They're poison reptiles, them. You remember what I tell you. But I don't say that we're all scalped . . . I simply say that we're wearin' mighty loose hair."

He pointed up. "Go look around the palisade at the old-timers. You'll always find some of the youngsters pining and aching for a fight. But if you see a grin on the face of a single old-timer, you come back here and tell me about it. It'll take a mighty weight off of my mind. But right now, the way I feel, we're gonna have our tongues hangin' out for water in about two days. After that, we'll march. And then God help us. The Indians will send out to every encampment within five hundred miles of us. They'll come swarmin' down. Where there is one red man now, there'll be ten before the finish."

"Then why not start the march immediately . . . now?" asked Tarlton with enthusiasm.

"What good is a little earlier start? They'll ramp along a hundred mile a day . . . we'll crawl ten with our wagons, if we got luck. They'll be back with their tribes before we get well started, anyways. You go tell Duncan that I want to know what he intends doin'. But right now, I wouldn't stack our chances ag'in' the price of this here bottle of phosphorus that the fool of an agent sent out to me." He took a small flask from his pocket, and then hurled it across the room with an oath of disgust.

Tarlton looked after it with blank eyes. Then suddenly he started up and took the flask. "You don't want this, Quigley?"

"I can get on right smart without it, son."

"I'll take it, then," said Tarlton.

"What kind of a thought have you got about it?"

"I don't know," said the gambler. "But the idea that I have might give us all one chance in a thousand."

"Which it would be a damn' fine thing to add that extra chance," said Quigley gravely. "Now, you go and find Duncan and ask him from me."

Tarlton went up to the old trader, and found him in the center of the fort yard, surrounded by half a dozen of the elders, in a serious consultation, but he broke off the talk as he saw Tarlton approach.

"We'll have no luck," he said, "while this thing is with us. As long as he's with us, I know which way the stick will be floating. Have you come up here to give us good advice, young man?"

Gloomy faces turned upon Tarlton. He said

shortly that he had come from Quigley to ask what measures were to be taken.

"Tell Quigley," said Duncan, "that when we know, we'll tell him, because every rifle in this here fort is going to be needed, whether the man that aims it is hurt or not. And those that can't handle a rifle," he said pointedly, "can sit back with the women and children and help to load." Then, after pausing briefly, he added: "Tell Quigley it's mostly up to what happens to Meany. If they murder him, they'll want to murder the rest of us. But if they don't taste blood . . . why, who knows?"

With that most unsatisfactory answer, Tarlton returned to Quigley and found him philosophically puffing at his pipe.

"It's as I said," said Quigley. "Will they kill Meany? Have they done it already? Who knows? Will they rush us tonight, or will they wait to starve us out? Oh, it's a pretty game, and we're settin' in the middle of it."

Tarlton returned no answer. He was sitting with downward head, his chin resting on his fist, staring into a corner, and the other, recognizing the profound abstraction of the boy, said nothing more.

The day went swiftly by, for it was the night the men in the fort dreaded. It was not until the sun hung on the very rim of the western sky, with swollen cheeks and a face of red gold, that

Tarlton stood up and held out his hand to the wounded man.

"Good bye," he said. "I'm riding out."

"Aye, you're apt to," said the other with a grunt of laughter, and Tarlton went up to the yard of the fort.

Two or three heavy columns of smoke were rising from the half-green wood of which the supper fires were built. On the walls were half a dozen men as sentinels. The rest were below in the yard, stirring in the tangle of wagons, moving slowly, like men who carried burdens.

From her stall, Tarlton took the mare, saddled her, groomed her, fitted the bit into her mouth, and she nosed his shoulder fondly. Then he led her out, mounted, and rode up to the gate.

Duncan stood beside it, smoking his long-stemmed pipe. "You're goin' out for a little canter, eh?" Duncan said with a sneer.

"I am," said Tarlton.

"You fool," said the trader. "I half believe that you would."

"I shall," said Tarlton, "if you'll open the gate enough to let me through."

"Why," said the other, "have we got a hero, here? Have we got a bright young hero to rise up and shine for the camp?"

"Will you open the gate?" asked Tarlton quietly.

Duncan stared, and then suddenly he roared. "Open the gate! I'll see the end of this bluff in about five seconds. Open the gate and let him out!"

There was a murmur of surprise, but the gate was obediently thrust open just enough to permit one horse to pass out. The men at the heavy wooden levers stood grinning at Tarlton, perfectly sure that he would not be so mad as to ride out into the open danger of the field.

He leaned, looked to the tightness of his cinch, and then pushed the mare deliberately through the gap and into the naked danger of the outdoors. There he rode straight down the slope toward the nearest encampment, which was that of the Crows, and right and left he saw groups of young braves who were circling the plain now rein in their horses and look toward him. In another moment, some of them began to drift cautiously up the slope, to cut off his return.

XIII

The sky was wild and grand. All toward the west, there was a clear arch, filled with the red-gold light, but from the east a massive wall of darkness was riding up the heavens, and already had reached the zenith. It was a thunderstorm of magnificent dimensions, putting down long arms of mist that turned purple, and gleaming sapphire, and rosy gold as the sunset light streamed through them. They were like thin legs that strode forward, upholding the enormous weight of the storm above.

Tarlton looked up calmly at this approaching crisis in the sky. There was a greater storm of anxiety, and hope, and excitement in his own heart.

The river, reflecting the sunset on the one hand and the clouds on the other, was half crimson and half filled with thunderous masses of shadow, and the grass shuddered and parted as heavy blasts of wind struck it.

Before him, the wandering parties of Indians separated to either side, as though they were anxious to give him an open passage, although he knew perfectly that they were simply striving to entice him forward, and that the others were gathered at his back.

But he would not look behind him, or show the slightest apprehension. Only, when the mare stumbled heavily after putting her foot in a hole, he could look down and back and, by that glance, see the wall of the fort on that side lined with the slender black silhouettes of the garrison that had swarmed up there to watch the progress of this wild adventure. He wondered, with a grim smile, if Helen Meany were among the rest, and what her thoughts might be concerning the adventure? And, with that same backward glance, he saw the sudden sweep of young braves behind him, like arrows launched from many bows, and all aimed at him.

If he turned his head toward them, he knew, suddenly, that an actual volley of feathered shafts would drive through his body. He went straight on, therefore, at a soft jogging trot, his head high, his shoulders squared, in spite of the thunder of the hoofs beating behind him, and the swift shudders that passed through his back.

Before him, too, rapid riders were hurling themselves forward. They were nearer. They loomed suddenly before him, galloping wildly. Their yells tore the air, and he saw the gleaming of their weapons, spearheads, and arrows on the string.

The sun was down. The west was a torrent of crimson, a wall of fire that seemed to be bursting out toward the plain, toppling from the crest as water might topple.

And then the pursuit was upon him.

Terrific shouts tore at his ears. Arrows flashed past him. Spear points reached like lightning flashes across his shoulders, from either side, and descending hatchets made bright arcs of light glancing by his head.

Yet not a blow struck home!

Tarlton knew, then, that one instant of quailing would see his brains scattered in the grass. He, therefore, galloped forward, apparently unconcerned.

Those from the rear, passing forward, slipped through the flying ranks of those charging from the west. And then the whole mass whirled with shouts and threatening weapons around Tarlton.

This whirlwind parted, and through the midst of it appeared the broad shoulders and the ugly face of Rising Bird. The greeting between him and Tarlton was short and simple.

"Come, brother," said Rising Bird in the Blackfoot tongue, which he knew Tarlton understood. "The young men have been glad to see you. They have been showing you the edges of their knives and the points of their spears, to prove what friends the Crow nation can be. Come with me. There is a couch in my lodge prepared for you."

And he took Tarlton straight on and through the village to the center of it. A tangle of women, naked children, howling dogs, swarmed around them, but Rising Bird brushed these aside, and took Tarlton into a tall lodge in the last circle, a lodge ornamented with the crescent moon in yellow on a background of red and black. The stars, too, appeared in staggering brilliancy upon that naïve painting.

Inside, two squaws stood up to greet their lord and his guest. A boy of some eight years leaped in through the teepee flap, and stood erect, hands clenched at his sides, his eyes flashing at Tarlton. That was the son. He looked like a bird of prey about to pounce. But the lord of the teepee pointed Tarlton to a couch. Leaning against a costly back rest, he prepared the inevitable pipe, and the white man smoked, and passed it back.

"It is good," said Rising Bird, "that in one day two friends each can help the other. Which way will you ride away from this trouble?"

"I must ride as an Indian," said Tarlton, "and I ride for one night only."

"Brother," said the Crow, "I wish to be your friend not for one day, but for your life. Do not stop with one night. I myself shall ride with you until you are clear of the young men, because they are like hungry hawks, pursuing, and always on the wing. After I leave you, ride on and on." He picked up a little dust from the floor of the teepee and tossed it into the air. "Trouble spreads more quickly than fire," he said as the dust fanned out and puffed in the drafty air.

Tarlton could understand. "Has the fire gone far away?" he said.

"All day," answered the Crow chief, after a moment of hesitation, "as fast as a horse can run, trouble has flown off over the grass."

"Very well," said Tarlton. "I would be happy to go from this place, but that I cannot do. I am going to stay near my white friends in the fort. I am not going to do any harm to the Indians, either. But first, I must change my clothes."

The chief looked earnestly at him, and as he paused, the weight of the thunderstorm struck the camp with a great crashing. It was a powerful blast that instantly sucked the flames of the fire out sideways, and from without they heard the frantic yelling of unlucky squaws whose ill-secured teepees had been uprooted and sent flying by the gale, while the household possessions either were tumbled topsy-turvy, or else floated far away.

Rising Bird remained utterly unmoved by this commotion, except to look up calmly. Then he said: "The Sky People are very angry tonight, brother."

"They are angry with the Blackfeet," Tarlton said readily enough, "because they have seen how the Blackfeet have taken a friend who came to them meaning them no harm, and how they have held him. Perhaps they already have murdered him?"

"The trader?" said the Crow chief. "He is still alive." He said it gloomily, with his eyes upon the ground. Then he looked up and added: "Why should the Sky People be angry because of what the Indians do to the white men? Do the whites make sacrifices to them?"

Tarlton answered logically enough: "The truth is that the Sky People take note of goodness even to a dog. Then would they not watch goodness to other men?"

Rising Bird shrugged, and his nostrils expanded a little. He said: "We are good friends, my brother. Let us talk of other things, and of what will make you happy. Your people are not my people, and our spirits are not your spirits."

Tarlton did not persist. But he said: "I want very little. I want only a loincloth and moccasins. After that, I want two or three old robes and some help to cut them up so that they will fit over me and over my horse."

"Over you and your horse?" echoed the chief.

"This is a stratagem," said Tarlton. "It will do no harm to anyone. Last of all, I want the longest war spear that you own."

The chief pointed to it, extending high into the gloom of the tent, its point a glimmer of bright steel. "There are robes," he said. "Take the best. They are not good enough for my friend."

But Tarlton picked out only the three oldest and most tattered robes, worn thin and hairless. These, with the help of the two squaws—while Rising Bird looked curiously on—were fashioned to make leg stalls for the mare, and a shelter for her neck, head, and very tail, and a covering for Tarlton. It was a clumsy leather suit that could be fitted upon her. And yet it was roughed out so rapidly that the work did not take an hour.

As the women worked, the men ate, until the preparations were complete. Then the squaws were sent out, Tarlton stripped, put on the loin strap, the moccasins, and the buffalo robe, which covered him to the heels.

At that moment, a messenger came, spoke hastily to the Crow, and passed on.

Said Rising Bird: "Brother, I am called to the tents of the Blackfeet to take counsel with them there. By my advice, this is your time to ride fast and to ride far. The mare will not fail you. Her legs are long. But take two more of my horses, and change to them when the good mare grows tired."

"You are called to the Blackfeet," suggested Tarlton, "to advise them about the life of Meany, the trader from the fort. Brother, speak to save his life."

Rising Bird answered darkly: "I do not love the whites. Once, I was not alone. I had two strong brothers. I was the weakest and the poorest. I lived on the scraps that were left from their glory. I was famous in the tribe and became a chief only because we had the same father. Now they are gone. Their scalps were not taken by a Cheyenne, or by a Ute. They died under the guns of the white men. My heart is sore. I have one white brother. And that is all. I have opened my heart to him and given him good words. Let him be wise and accept them, and ride far away."

And they went out into the rain-racked darkness of the night.

XIV

In the camp of the Blackfeet, the life of Meany balanced nicely. He was not an inch from death at one time; he was verging toward safety at another, according as one party and then another secured the ascendancy.

First, dragged up roughly to the camp by the Blackfeet youths, the latter were willingly dispersed by a rush of the Blackfeet women, who seized on Meany and would have made him a victim forthwith. For, by this time, there was not a tribe in the mountains or over the plains which had not certain victims to mourn at the hands of the whites. And, with true Indian instinct, they blamed upon the entire white "tribe" their losses.

Meany would have been slain by the women with the most dreadful torments if Spotted Calf himself, at this point, had not intervened. He was a young chief. He had a young man's bitter impulses, but he was enough of a statesman to understand that it was a dangerous affair to involve his tribe with the white men.

At last, he freed the white man from the circle of the women, and saw that he was convoyed to a lodge near his. It was a sort of overflow lodge, or guest house, attached to his own, and it had served before this to accommodate prisoners of importance. Then Spotted Calf called an assemblage of his own chiefs.

The young leaders and the old came. The medicine men opened the ceremony with due solemnity. After that, they argued about the proper fate for Meany the trader, and the vote was for death. It was by the treachery of his council that they had lost so many goods that day. It was, however, for more important reasons that he was to die. And one after another the Blackfeet arose and spoke of young warriors found dead in the hills—how often shot through the back, killed as by an Indian with craft, scalped as by an Indian, but the slayer leaving the tracks of moccasins such as an Indian never would have been wearing.

But before this debate was ended, one of the oldest men gave this bit of toothless wisdom. "If you strike, strike at the heart . . . but if you strike, let it be all together. The Blackfeet are a great people. They are the greatest of the peoples of the world. But still we will need help to beat the whites. Send for the Crows and the Cheyennes. They are great warriors. Show them our hearts and ask them if they will charge at our sides."

To this, Spotted Calf willingly assented. He, by instinct, guessed at the wisdom behind that advice.

But he waited through the day. He was willing that the skirmishing out on the plain around the fort should grow hotter and hotter. If by any chance an Indian should be fired upon and killed, then without a doubt the decision of the council would turn in only one way.

But dusk came—the thunderstorm smote all the camps—and still there was no word of a serious casualty before the fort, where the fire of the rifles was being sternly kept silent by wise Duncan.

So, with the darkness, Spotted Calf saw no more reason for delaying the council, and now he did two things. First, he dispatched six young braves, as vigilant as hawks, to press up through the darkness and lie near the fort, ready to mark any attempt on the part of the whites to escape through the storm. Then he sent out his invitation to the chief men of both the neighboring encampments, and they quickly gathered in his own capacious lodge.

Twenty head men of the three nations now sat shoulder to shoulder in a circle, so much so that when the council was opened, and the first man spoke in the person of the oldest—an ancient Crow—this venerable orator burst out: "Here are three great people, all side-by-side, heart touching heart, arm touching arm, peaceful and happy together. Oh, that we should steal across the plains, hunting for the lives of one another. If we were at peace, if we were as one, we could sweep all the world before us. As for the life of this white man, that is a small thing, and no doubt it has been forfeited. Let us pour out his blood. Let us make it a sacrifice to the Sky People, who surely hate the whites. After that sacrifice, we will all be tied together. The Crows, the Blackfeet, and the Cheyennes will make one great nation. We will drive the Sioux into the northern snows and take their hunting grounds. Then we will conquer the Comanches, and have all the world at our knees. All this I see in promise, as I see you sitting here, shoulder to shoulder."

The wind had fallen, and though the rain fell in crashing torrents and the thunder beat like the striking of huge, half-muffled wings in the distance, still, at intervals, Meany in the little adjoining lodge could hear enough of the discourse to make out its meaning, and his flesh prickled with fear.

This old fire-eater was followed by a more peaceful spirit, a Crow.

He began by saying that he did not doubt the good heart and the strong wit of his fellow tribesman, but he knew that at other times alliances had been made to strike the whites. They always failed. He did not know why, but he argued against war, because in the hands of the Indians it never had been a successful weapon against the whites.

Then the debate raged freely on both sides.

At one point, it was suggested that it would be of importance to find out what the prisoner would give, if anything, as a ransom for his life, and he was led into the lodge to give his answer for himself.

It was a ticklish moment for Meany. His keen, understanding eyes pierced through the swirling smoke and rested upon the hard faces of the chiefs, and he knew that they were against him, one and all. Yet he dared not speak with too much emotion. It would have disgusted the Indians to think that he was pleading for his life too passionately. He must rather speak in measured tones, as a businessman. If he even put too high a value upon himself, he would be considered a braggart and a coward, and probably given at once to the terrible hands of the women—torturers to whom the Spanish Inquisition was as nothing.

Therefore, he offered them, in the mildest of speeches, a good horse, worthy of a charge in war, or the running of the buffalo, to every chief assembled there. Also, he would give with every horse as many beads as his doubled hands could hold. This, he said, he gave not so much as a price on his head, but because he was eager that the trading should begin, and because he wanted to show the Indians that he prized them, and, furthermore, that now he could tell which men among the three nations were well worthy of honoring.

Hardly had the flap of the teepee closed behind him as he was led out when he heard Little Bull, the Cheyenne chief, rising to advise that the offer should be taken.

Said Little Bull: "You speak a great deal of the white men, though what have you seen of them? Would you judge the Comanches by the few warriors who have happened to wander north, and who live with us, now and then, in our teepees during a winter? No, you would not judge their power by these men, who often are outcasts, and have no real strength or worth. But we know, besides, from men who have ridden far south and seen them, that the Comanches are a great people, the richest in horses of any in the world.

"How do we see the white men wander forth here? We do not see single men who come forth and rest for the winter in our teepees. But we see men who come forth in small groups, each man loaded down with wealth, and each man eager for more. They do not have to skulk in their teepees. They build their forts so cunningly and so strongly that these forts are able to stand off the attack of the best warriors of an Indian nation. Not with one force would we attack this fort, for instance. We have to take council together, and three great nations pour down on one place.

"But are these all the white men? They have few women and almost no children with them.

Where their masses of tribesmen are will be where they have left their women and their children.

"I, Little Bull, know the thing that I speak of. The great river which we call The Father of the Waters, and which we think of as far, far in the east, is to them far west. Beyond this great flood, they live in great cities of lodges built of wood, and of stone, and of baked mud. These people are so many that, if all the Indians of all the prairies were to gather together in one force and attack the whites, they could not win.

"It is best for us to live as freely as we can, but within a limit. Let us do nothing that will make so much trouble and so much noise that the story of it will go across the great river and come to the ears of all the other whites. Let us do nothing that will reach the ears of their chiefs, where they sit together smoking on the shore of the eastern ocean.

"If, now and then, the red men destroy a small party of traders, it is no matter. No sound of it as loud as the voice of a bird in the wind that comes to the fathers of the white people, far away. But such a thing as this, and the killing of many white men in a fort, will anger them. They will send out thousands of warriors. They will come up the rivers in fire canoes deep into the heart of our country.

"And even if they do not find us, some of them will stay. Then others and others will come.

Wherever they come, they will hold some land. They will grow in numbers. Even now, they begin to push out fingers into the heart of our land. Let us leave them alone. Let us take each of us a good horse and the double handful of beads. This is what I think it wise to do."

When Little Bull sat down, it was plain that his speech had daunted the hearts of half the chiefs, and Meany waited, his heart beating frantically with hope in the next lodge.

All was quiet for a long moment, and then a vast peal of thunder burst from the heavens above them, and, as its echoes went bounding and crackling down, the first of all the speakers shouted suddenly: "The Sky People hear those words, and they are angry. They threaten us with their contempt unless we strike at the white men. Are we cowards to do what the Sky People command us to? Look, look!"

With this, he rushed to the flaps of the lodge and threw them wide, and the whole assemblage saw above them the rush of a lightning flash, plunging out of the high masses of the clouds.

XV

It was exactly at this critical moment that a little boy on the outskirts of the village of the Blackfeet ran out of his father's lodge in order to look up at the skies and see if a portion of them had not fallen in the last great thunder crash. He looked up and saw that great thunderbolt careering through the sky like a white ship, like a white rider of Blackfeet lore. And, at the same time, he heard the loud chant of criers running through the camp and calling out the warriors. He listened, his heart beating with fear and with joy, when at that moment a strange rider appeared through the night beside him.

This man was an apparition that seemed to be on fire. And so was the horse he rode on.

The little boy would have run away with a cry of fear, but hands caught him and lifted him to the pommel of the saddle.

After all, the man was not actually on fire. But edgings of light appeared around the verge of his robe. And the horse itself was outlined with a strange glow from within and appeared, in fact, to be covered with garments like those that cover a man.

The boy had not much time to wonder at this apparition, when he was much reassured by hearing a voice speak to him in good Blackfoot, saying: "Little brother, I have come in from a long march, brought by the messengers. Therefore, tell me the teepee of Spotted Calf."

"It is there in the center of the lodges," said the boy. "It is there at the foot of that hill."

For there was a mound in the middle of the camp, a high mound of earth, and at the foot of this the chief had built his teepee.

"That is good," said the stranger to the boy. "And where is the dog of a white man who was brought into the camp this same day?"

"Beside the lodge of Spotted Calf there is a small teepee. There you will find him. And who are you, stranger and brother?"

"I," said the stranger after the slightest hesitation, "am only a skirmisher, come before the remainder of the Blackfeet who will arrive today, all eager."

He dropped the boy, and the latter stood back. It seemed to him that he had noticed an odd, stifling odor, when he was close to this rider from the heart of the night. It seemed to him, also, that faint fumes arose, but of this he could not be sure, because the horseman did not pause any longer, but rode straight on through the thick of the camp.

Twisting here and there, this man from the dark proceeded through the camp, which was now filling with hurrying men who went back and forth, gathering toward the center of the camp, every man mounted on his best war pony, and every man armed with the choicest of his weapons. For the criers had circulated everywhere through the village of the Blackfeet, and all the warriors, young and old, had answered the call.

Out from the lodge of Spotted Calf the chiefs of the three nations had come, and they had paused for a moment to watch the muster of the Piegans.

The Blackfeet came in throngs, tall, magnificently made men, with long hair flowing freely over their shoulders—hair that was whipped straight out now by the pressure of the wind. And as they gathered in a thick mass at the center of the camp, waiting for the command of their leader, a sudden wild voice ran screaming upon them carried by fear.

"The white rider and the horse of fire! Look! Look!"

And they looked up to the top of the little hill and there they were able to see a dreadful figure against the black and moving sky of the night. At that very moment as they looked, it happened that a huge lightning bolt burst from the clouds and angled toward the earth. The startled warriors could not be sure whether they had seen the apparition of the flaming horse before or after the lightning bolt, and to most of them it seemed as though they had seen the thunderbolt drive down from the sky and appear upon the earth in the form of a man of white fire on a horse of white flame. For every detail of that rider on the hilltop was bathed in brilliant light. And yet the light shone on nothing else around him.

He was naked except for a loincloth. And the loincloth alone was dark. That, and the moccasins upon his feet, and the feathers in his hair. But all the rest of this celestial warrior flamed. His hair blew over his shoulders like a garment of fire. And the horse burned, likewise, and even the bridle was a bridle of white fire, held by the burning hand of the rider.

Most marvelous of all, this rider bore in his hand a great long spear, and now he turned his horse, and he lowered that spear of heavenly fire and with it he pointed straight at the lodge of Spotted Calf, in the midst of the Blackfeet.

When the tribesmen saw this, a universal groan went up from them, and the strongest warriors there were not ashamed to shrink and groan in the agony of their fear, for the old tribal story rang in every ear, as they had heard it in their childhood.

Then that rider began to move down the hillside, and a wild cry went up from every throat when it was seen that the print of his hoofs upon the earth was outlined in living fire that quivered, and trembled, and turned green. And all the way from the top of the hill to the bottom, it was observed that the footprints remained as clearly imprinted as though the fire were welling up from the earth.

At that, with a deep cry of terror, the horde swept backward. And they huddled together, ready to flee in the utmost fright, and pressing close to one another in the extremity of their fear.

Still they remained to look, and the greatness of their astonishment and their curiosity was such that they were almost more delighted with unearthly pleasure in the sight of the vision than they were overwhelmed with awe.

Many things were noted, about which all agreed the next day.

There were some who said that a cloud of livid smoke curled upward above the stranger from the sky, and floated toward the heaven from which he had descended to this fortunate earth. But in this, all would not agree. Only the women were unanimous, as they always were in making each feature of this wonder more miraculous.

There were some who declared that it was plainly seen that the horse galloped through the sky, bursting from among the clouds, and that it raced down in three long leaps to the earth, just as the fall of the thunderbolt will make three jags.

But most agreed that at the moment when the horse smote the earth, the ground trembled, and immediately afterward there was such a great peal of thunder as never had been heard before. The whole tribe were willing to swear to this detail.

It was further said that the eyes of the stranger shot forth burning sparks, and the direction of his glance was always marked by a ghostly stream of light. But there was much divergence about this, and many said that the mouth and the eyes of the stranger were dark.

What all could swear to was that the point of the dreadful spear dripped living fire, and that some of that fire fell upon the ground, and that there it burned terribly, with a small immortal light.

Now this celestial visitor moved down the hillside and rode straight to the lodge that cowered close beside the lodge of the chief, Spotted Calf. There he dismounted and walked forward, and the prints of his moccasins were fire upon the earth.

He laid his hand upon the flap and cast it back, and the finger mark was a mark of fire that did not burn. He entered that small teepee, and there was a groan of anguish from the Blackfeet. Was it on account of the white man that this messenger had been sent from the Sky People?

Yes, for behold. Out from the teepee stepped the divine rider, and with him walked Meany, the trader. And the rider went down the slope toward the river, and his burning hand was upon the head of Meany in sign of protection, and yet Meany could stand the fire.

Then the Blackfeet warriors smote their hands against their foreheads and looked again at this marvel, and every man told himself that he was dreaming.

But that dream went down to the river and entered the water. And, at that moment, came the greatest miracle of all. For the heavens opened and there was a great shaft of lightning. And there were some who swore that the lightning descended from the heavens to the earth, near the river, but all who had eyes and sense were able to see that the flash rose from the river to the heavens.

And there were some—chiefly among the old women—whose eyes were so keen that they were able to distinguish the form of the horse of fire as it fled upward, glancing as swift as light.

But this much was certain, that when the rider came to the river, after the blinding flash of lightning, he and Meany disappeared, and on the water's face appeared a great glowing spot, which floated slowly down with the current, and disappeared around the next bend of the river.

That was the last that was seen of the miracle.

The Blackfeet hurried back to their teepees. All the night they made medicine and offered prayers and made vows of sacrifice. Then, the visiting chiefs from the council went back to their own peoples and told what they had seen, and every Crow and every Cheyenne gave thanks that they were not as the Blackfeet, under the wrath of the Sky People.

The next morning, a few of the most daring spirits climbed the hill and there they found what looked like strange garments of leather, clumsily cut. The meaning of this was not understood. But certainly men could see the prints of the hoofs of a horse, leading down from the crest straight to the door of the prisoner's lodge.

XVI

The next morning, in the earliest dawn, though the thunderstorm had passed, the three nations hastily struck their lodges and prepared to march, when a messenger came out from the fort.

He was the half-breed, Young River, and he said to the Indians that the heart of Meany was compassionate, that he had interceded with the flaming rider from heaven and had induced him to promise that, although the sin of the Blackfeet had been great in taking advantage of the person of a helpless man, moreover of a favorite of heaven, yet now at the request of Meany the Blackfeet and their allies would be wholeheartedly forgiven.

Meany himself would forgive. He sent that

assurance to all the chiefs, and above all to Spotted Calf. If they wished to open the trading now, he, Meany, would be glad to have them do so, on the basis of a cup of sugar to one buffalo robe.

Furthermore, he desired to say that where the hand of the fiery messenger had rested upon his head, some of the celestial fire still glowed, and though it was dim and not visible in the daylight, in a darkened teepee he, Meany, would show to the greatest of the chiefs the sign of the fire still burning upon his hair.

They went down in wonder, and the greatest chiefs were duly admitted, and the crowd was gathered into a big darkened lodge in a corner of the fort. Then Meany took off his hat, and it was seen that upon his hair, visibly imprinted in pale fire, was the mark of the five fingers of a hand.

From that moment Meany became a colossal figure, a legendary form.

From that moment, there was not an Indian of the plains who would not sooner have cut off his own hand than offend the mysterious favorite of the Sky People, whose favor had been so visibly shown to them in the camp of the Blackfeet.

That day the trading was very brisk. Floods of robes, of beaver pelts, poured into the fort. There was nothing but good feeling on all sides. The Indians felt that a great clemency had been shown to them all, and they made no hard points in the trading. The whites themselves were more than a little overawed.

For, from the top of the palisade, more than one watcher had seen, with a sinking heart, that form of white fire ride down, and disappear in the river. Some said one thing, and some said another, but upon the whole there was an air of mystery attached to Meany from that day forth, even among the white men of the frontier. They were almost as superstitious as the Indians, if the truth be told.

Certainly there was no getting away from one truth—that Meany had been captured by the Blackfeet, that the fort had been in the utmost peril, that his life had been despaired of by Meany himself—and that then by a figure of fire he was led forth to safety.

But, except to an Indian, it was a matter on which Meany never would utter a word. His lips were sealed.

But after that first day's trading, a group of five gathered in the room where Quigley lay wounded. In that group was Duncan, and Meany himself, and Helen his daughter, and Quigley, of course, and lastly young Tarlton, who was miraculously restored to the good graces of both Meany and Duncan.

Said Duncan: "Now, young man, you can go out and tell this story around, and it'll get you a famous name for one of the slickest tricks, and the coolest-headed, if not the smartest, that ever I heard of in the stories of the whole frontier. But I'd wait till the trading with these tribes is over, if I was you."

And Meany said with feeling: "Aye, wait till that is over. There's a fortune in this day, my son. The Blackfeet are pouring out their plews like water, and asking almost nothing in exchange. My skin room is overflowing. I've never seen such furs."

Then Tarlton answered with his usual cynical lightness: "The point is, my friends, that it's dangerous for a man to speak lightly of the fires from heaven." And he took a flask from his pocket. "But there's still a little touch of the stuff left in here. I used up almost all of it, and put the last big daub on the head of the spear. Confound me if the stuff didn't run off the steel and drip on the ground. And those Blackfeet groaned like so many frightened demons. But perhaps you'd better take this flask and keep the phosphorus that's left in it. Because there's no telling . . . you may get in a tight pinch again. But now that you've got a chummy reputation as a friend of the Sky People, you can always show the mark of their hand on your head. The rest of the time, you'd better keep on your hat."

That was advice that Meany kept to the end of his life, so that day and night a hat always was clamped upon his head. And the mystery never left him—at least in the eyes of the Indians. And that mystery, with good, native, Yankee thrift, he converted into a fortune of handsome proportions.

What came of Tarlton?

Young Helen Meany had designs upon him. Because she saw that not only was this youth agreeable and different from others, but also he stood high in the councils of her father, and literally he had given life back to the trader when life was forfeit. Even stern-faced Duncan had so utterly relented that he insisted upon taking Tarlton's goods and driving with them such prodigious bargains with the Indians that the fortune of Tarlton was at least restored to what it should have been when he departed from the river.

However, Tarlton took all these things lightly. For it is to be feared that he was a light-minded young man. And perhaps Helen Meany looked a trifle less beautiful to him as soon as he saw that he could have her.

At any rate, it is useless to make surmises, and it is safer to tell the truth even when it cannot be fully comprehended.

For as they walked forth before the fort, on a day toward the end of the trading, Tarlton paused and pointed down at the camp of the Cheyennes. It was growing deep into the dusk of the day, and every transparent teepee glowed with the fire that burned within.

"Helen," said the young man, "if I ever have a home, I think it will have to be a home like that."

"A home like that!" cried the girl. "A wretched tent?"

"Ah, does it look like that to you?" he said dreamily.

"You don't mean that you'd go to live in a tribe of wild savages, David?" she said.

"Savages?" said Tarlton. "Well . . . I don't know. They look like free men to me."

And the very day after the trading ended, when the Cheyennes disappeared, David Tarlton disappeared with them, all his possessions being deftly moved away by his half-breed companion, Young River. And Fort Meany saw the flaming rider from the sky no more.

Outlaw Buster

"Outlaw Buster" appeared in the August, 1937 issue of *Complete Western Book Magazine*, and features one of Faust's gentle giants, Barney Dwyer, a social outcast with more brawn than brain, who has yet to find a place in the world despite his efforts to do what is right. It is the third and final story in the Barney Dwyer saga that began with "The Quest" which appeared in the May, 1933 issue of *West* and was collected in *The Quest* (Five Star Western, 2009). The second Dwyer story, "The Trail of the Eagle" which appeared in the July, 1933 issue of *West*, is collected in *Outlaws From Afar* (Five Star Westerns, 2007).

I

From the window of the hotel, Sheriff Jim Elder pointed out the Coffeeville jail. It was a little white frame building with a roof painted green.

"We've got 'em there for the minute, Barney," he said to Dwyer, "but if you refuse to appear against 'em, we probably can't hold 'em long. Not unless I can get one of McGregor's gang to turn state's evidence against his boss."

"Suppose that I go into court and tell what I know about Adler and McGregor?" he said.

"Adler will get enough years to make it life, for him . . . and they'll hang McGregor," said the sheriff instantly. "And with McGregor gone, we'll have peace through the whole range."

Barney Dwyer put his hands together and twisted them so hard that his shoulder muscles leaped out and filled the slack of his blue flannel shirt as a hard wind fills a sail. There was trouble in his eyes, pain wrinkling the center of his brow.

"I can't do it, Jim," he said. "I know they're bad ones, that pair. But if a man were hanged because of what I said in a courtroom, it would be poison to me."

The sheriff exclaimed impatiently: "What would they do to you, if they managed to get out of that jail, Barney? Tell me that?"

"They'd murder me if they could," said Barney. "I know that. I'm afraid of 'em, too. But to hang a man with the words I speak . . . I couldn't do it."

The sheriff had many reasons for respecting Barney Dwyer, but now he stared with a mounting fury into that gentle, simple, troubled face. Words to voice all his anger came up into the throat of Jim Elder, but he choked them suddenly back. He turned his back sharply on big Barney Dwyer and made two rapid turns up and down the room. When he halted again in front of Barney, he snapped: "Will you talk to Sue Jones before you make up your mind?"

"I'll talk to her," agreed Dwyer. "But even Sue couldn't change my mind about this, I'm afraid. I'm going out to see her now at Doctor Swain's. The doctor says that he can cure her shoulder so that there'll hardly be a sign of a scar. Think of that!"

"Think of the beast that fired the bullet at a woman," said the sheriff. "Think of that . . . and think what it will mean to the range to put Adler and McGregor either in a hemp rope or behind the bars for life. I've spent years trying to hunt them down. After all my trying, you caught McGregor. It was a great thing. That's why that crowd is hanging around the hotel to see you. It was a wonderful thing that you did, Barney. But unless you follow it up with testimony in the courtroom, what you've done is as good as nothing."

The same pain came into the face of Dwyer, but he shook his head, slowly, and the sheriff knew, with despair, that nothing could budge him. Instead of answering directly, Barney Dwyer stepped gingerly toward the window and looked down into the street.

Men lingered on the verandah of the General Merchandise Store and more men were talking and laughing under the roof of the hotel porch, as well. New arrivals constantly galloped up, tied their horses at the long hitching rack, and, before entering the barroom or joining the others on the verandah, paused for a moment to look at the red mare, near to which none of the other animals were tethered. She herself was not tied, but she remained as though she were bound to the spot, switching her tail at the flies, sometimes swinging her head about to frighten them from her shoulders, sometimes stamping deeper holes in the dust with her forehoofs.

"D'you mean that they've come into Coffeeville to see me?" asked Barney Dwyer, his eyes growing round.

"You and the mare, yes," said the sheriff. "And all the women in the town are trying to get past Missus Swain to have a look at Sue. The Swain house is filled with pies, and fresh fish, and flowers, and everything the ladies of Coffeeville can think of that may get them past the front door of the house. Well, it's no wonder. Sue is the heroine, and you're the hero, Barney. You'll have a crowd at your heels the rest of your life, after the things you've done. And I hope the crowd bothers you as much as the flies are bothering your mare, down there."

There was a good-humored petulance in his voice as he spoke. But Barney Dwyer held up a protesting hand.

"I'm no hero, Jim," he said. "I was frightened, too, a lot of times. I was terribly frightened, as a matter of fact. I . . . I . . . how can I get away from that crowd, Jim? Will you tell me? I've got to see Sue, but I can't wade through all those people and . . ."

He blushed, with misery in his eyes he appealed to the sheriff, but Jim Elder merely grinned.

"You've made your medicine, and you'll have to swallow it," he said.

"No!" exclaimed Barney Dwyer. "I could go down the back way."

"What back way?" asked the sheriff.

Barney pointed to the window at the rear of the room. Then he picked up a forty-foot rope that hung on the back of a chair, neatly coiled, and carried it to the back window. There was a long drop beneath him to the yard below, which was walled about by a high board fence. Barney tied one end of the rope firmly to a chair.

"Are you going to take the risk of breaking your neck," demanded Jim Elder angrily, "for the sake of avoiding that gang, which only wants to shake hands with you and buy you drinks?"

"Whiskey makes my head buzz around and around as though there were flies inside it," said Barney. "And yet if I don't take a drink men are angry. It hurts their pride. And then there's apt to be fighting, and I hate a fight, Jim. You see how it is?"

The sheriff peered at him as though he were a great distance off; he peered as a man does when the glare of the desert is hurting the eyes.

"You beat me, Barney!" he exclaimed. "But in the name of God, let me try to make you see reason before you break your back falling out of a hotel window. You admit that McGregor has done everything he can to put you out of the way. He's jailed you in his cellar. He's turned loose his gang to kill you. He's brought that old devil of a Doc Adler into the business to wreck you. He's even put his hands on Sue and taken her away from you. I'm asking you to remember that every low trick a man can use on another man, he's tried on you. And all I'm asking of you, is to take that devil out of the world by simply standing up in a courtroom and telling the truth as the law requires you to do. It's not even vengeance. It's justice. It's doing your duty to the world."

Barney Dwyer paused to consider, with his

head raised, and his mild eyes contemplating his thought. Slowly his big head began to shake from side to side in denial.

"Maybe you're right, Jim," he said at last. "You know a lot more than I do. A whole lot more. But I'll tell you something . . . once I had McGregor in my hands, and I was killing him. I went blind with the joy of killing him, till Sue stopped me. Afterward, I was sick. My heart was sick to think I'd been acting like a beast. I've seen a wildcat killing a mountain grouse, tearing it. I must have been like that. And afterward, I swore that I'd never lift a hand against any man, except to defend myself. And I won't lift my voice, either, Jim. Not even in a courtroom."

The sheriff groaned, made a gesture of surrender with both hands, and said no more. Barney Dwyer was already through the window. He wedged the chair carefully, threw out the length of the rope, and then went down it, hand over hand, rapidly. The two hundred pounds of his weight was a mere nothing, depending from the power of his arms.

The sheriff leaned out and watched. He saw the red bandanna fluttering at the neck of Dwyer. Near the bottom of the rope, he saw Barney pause for a moment to consider his landing place, holding by one hand to the rope as easily as an ape. And the sheriff bit his lip with wonder. Then Barney loosed his grip and dropped lightly.

He looked up and waved a cheerful hand at the sheriff, smiling.

"He makes no more of that circus trick," grunted the sheriff, "than I'd make of walking across the room. He's different from the rest of us, body and brain. Plain different."

Barney Dwyer had turned to the high board fence. There was no gate or door through it. So he leaped up, caught the upper rim, and so swung himself lightly over and dropped onto the sun-burned grass of the farther side.

It was a little winding lane that led down to the side of Coffee Creek. He glanced up and down it, and sighed as he made sure that there was no one in sight. He was wrong. A lad with a home-made rod in one hand, and a small string of fish in the other, was drifting slowly up the slope, under the deep shadow of the trees, and, seeing Barney, he had paused at once, to stare.

Now Barney tilted back his head and whistled three quick, sharp notes. After that he waited. The red mare would hear that call; the red mare would come at once, when she located the direction of the whistle. And he waited for her with his head thrown back, smiling a little in expectation. With her speed and grace under him, he would soon be far from the annoyance of crowds.

He heard the whinny of the mare, as familiar to him as the voice of a human to another man. Then another voice shot up close by, the yell of a boy who cried: "He's here! Come quick! Barney Dwyer! Barney Dwyer!"

That voice jumped with electric tinglings along the nerves of Barney. He turned, and, as he turned, he saw the boy come at him. The fishing rod was dropped, and the string of little silver fish tumbled into the dust.

"Barney Dwyer! I've got Barney! He's here! Hurry up, everybody!"

The freckled face of the lad was convulsed with delight. How many men in all the world would have dared to rush in this manner upon the famous might of Dwyer? But the boy had no fear. He dodged the surprised and outstretched hands of Barney, and caught at his belt.

"Barney Dwyer!" he shrieked. "I've caught Barney! Hurry!"

With one hand, Barney lifted the wriggling youngster by the nape of the neck. The terrible grasp of the other hand he laid on the wrist of the boy, trying to pull his grip loose. But he was afraid to use his strength. Even the iron-hard bones of grown men were apt to snap under his hold. Therefore he went gingerly about the work of detaching the grip of the boy.

And the youngster yelled louder than ever.

Here at last came the red mare, though late. And Barney could see that she limped. He was horrified. He looked again, and he saw that an iron band had been hammered into place around her left foreleg. It jounced up and down and made her gallop shorten to a hobble. While behind her, led by her going, streamed the head of the mob, rushing straight down upon Barney Dwyer.

II

Sweat broke out on the face of Barney Dwyer. He groaned to the clinging weight of the boy: "Let me go. I'll give you a good Twenty-Two rifle, if you'll let go. . . . I don't want to hurt you."

The boy glanced up at him with a fierce joy. "I've got Barney! Hurry!" he shrieked.

The people in the head of the mob came without shame disturbing them. And what a mob. There were young men dashing at the head of it, and, when they saw Barney, they gave tongue like dogs, and they made spy-hops into the air, like rabbits running from a foe. Behind them came children, grown men of dignity, and those people who abandon their dignity the last of any in a city—the girls of marriageable age, who usually walk with a conscious slowness, looking straight before them, aware with every nerve of the eyes of men. But even these were in the outskirts of the crowd, and so were the elder matrons, picking up their skirts in front of their fat knees, and laughing, and panting, and blushing with the speed of their running.

"Let me go!" groaned Barney, more desperately than ever, and, putting forth a little more of his strength, he plucked the boy from him.

The red mare was there, but her coming was too late. He could not leap into the saddle and ride her away, as a dead leaf rides an autumn gale. Not while that loop of iron was rattling up and down along her foreleg, threatening to lame her.

And directly behind her came the crowd. It spilled around Barney. He looked up from the agony of his embarrassment, and saw that the wicked sheriff remained in the rear window of the hotel, and laughed, and from that window the snaky length of the rope still dangled in the air, to betray the means of his retreat.

Instantly he felt that he had made a fool of himself, and he prayed with all of his heart that the word of this might not suddenly be carried to Sue Jones, so that she would be forced to smile faintly and sadly, as he had seen her smiling more than once already. She could always forgive him for his follies; she always would. But that made the pain no less.

They were all about him, the mob. The freckle-faced boy of the fishing rod was dancing up and down, laughing at a furious rate, clapping his hands together.

Some of the people had cameras. They began to call out to one another to get out of the way. They began to yell out, and exclaim.

A big man came laboring up among the last. He was white, a cellar white, a prison white, and he was patched with the red of effort. He wore a blue suit, and yellow-spotted blue silk necktie. He had spats over his low shoes. He had a golden watch chain draped across the large swell of his stomach.

He came through the rest like a great old-fashioned galleon that rides slowly, staggering among the swift waves. He panted exceedingly, poking before him with a polished cane in order to clear the way. When he was near enough he put a fat, wet hand upon the shoulder of Barney Dwyer.

"Came here . . . all the way . . . got news . . . good news . . . lucky boy," he said.

He really spoke as one capable of bestowing benefits. And the other people, nearby, actually cleared a circle and pushed back one against the other. They acted as though they knew that something more than curiosity had brought this man, at least. And they contented themselves with exclaiming noisily, and with lifting their cameras to get better angles on Barney.

His embarrassment rose to enormous proportions.

The fat man in the blue suit and the silken shirt took off his hat. He mopped the wet and rosy baldness of his head with one hand, and with the hat made eloquent gestures.

141

"Lucky, lucky boy," he said. "I'm from the Armitages Vaudeville Circuit. I'm a booking agent from them. I'm Isaac Baldwin. I've come to give you a contract . . . a good, fat contract. No more punching of cows at ten dollars a week. I'm offering you a contract signed on the line for a hundred dollars a week for a whole year. I'm offering you a fortune, Barney Dwyer!"

The mention of such a huge salary made other people speechless. Even the women forgot to snap photographs. Generally $1 a day was not bad pay on a ranch, during many seasons of the year, and how many cowpunchers worked out the winter months merely for board?

Isaac Baldwin went on: "That's not all. I'm offering you a whole lot more. I'm offering you *two* hundred . . . mind you . . . two hundred dollars a week, the instant that the charming girl who went through the dangers with you . . . two hundred dollars . . . the minute she puts her signature under yours. That's more than ten thousand dollars a year. You can marry, on that. Ten thousand dollars a year! Ha?"

"For what?" asked Barney, the mention of such a figure beginning to work like wild fire through his brain.

"For what? For simply walking on the stage and doing a little song and dance. I've got the song in my head already. I know the men to write it up and do the words, too. Bernie Falkenstein is the man."

"But I can't sing. I can't dance," said Barney.

"*Anybody* can sing and dance for ten thousand a year," said Isaac Baldwin. "It don't matter how you do it, does it? All the folks want to see is you and the girl. That's all they wanna see. A little front stage scene. Western. Mountains painted on the backdrop. You come in. Two guns. Sombrero, chaps, silver conchos, and all that. By God, I've got it better still. You lead the red mare with you. Everybody goes crazy. Everybody knows about you and the red mare. We'll throw in fifty dollars a week for the red mare, too."

"I don't know what you mean," Barney said gently.

"Yeah, you know all right," said Baldwin. "You mean you want more money? Whatcha call more money? I'm willing to talk business."

Another man came rushing from the distance. He was as lean as Isaac Baldwin was fat. He had grey side whiskers that fluffed out at the side of his face. He was dressed so noisily that it was apparent that he did not care how many people looked at him.

"Don't do no business with Baldwin! Don't do no business with Ickey!" he yelled through his nose. His voice was a nasal trumpet. "I'm from the Morpheum! Wait till you hear from me! Wait till you hear our terms."

He rushed right in through the crowd, and the people gave way before him, as though he were a plowshare and they the soil. He was talking money, and big money.

"Three hundred a week for you and the girl . . . a little song and dance number," he said. "I'm Jakie Blattman from the Morpheum booking office. Don't listen to them pikers of the Armitage! Listen to me. We're your friend. We're gonna do right by you."

"That's right. They'll do you proper!" yelled fat Isaac Baldwin. "The pikers! I'm gonna offer you four hundred a week . . . *and* all expenses. You two and the mare, besides. The famous Barney Dwyer and his red mare. All in headlines. All in the biggest electric signs that we can get. And his sweetheart . . . Sue Jones . . . the sweetheart of the Western World. D'you hear me?"

"The dirty piker!" yelled Blattman. "I'm talkin' to you, boy! Five hundred . . . six hundred dollars a week . . ."

"A thousand dollars a week!" screamed Isaac Baldwin, turning crimson and purple in his excitement, and his vocal efforts.

"Don't offer any more money," said Barney. "People might come to look at us. But we don't want to be looked at. Not for a *million* dollars a week. We couldn't talk to you about business. I'm sorry."

Baldwin turned furiously on Blattman. "You

done it, Blattman!" he roared. "You spoiled everything. I could've got him on a cheap, quiet little contract, and you spoiled it all. You went and spoiled it, you did. A pig is what you are. Listen, Mister Dwyer," he went on, whining to Barney, "I'm gonna make you our top offer for yourself and the mare and the girl . . . fifteen hundred dollars a week . . . which is fifty months' salary as a cowpuncher for you every week of your life. Fifteen hundred dollars . . ."

"Sixteen hundred . . . !" screamed Blattman.

"Not for sixteen million!" thundered Barney Dwyer. "Get out of here, will you!"

At that unexpected lion's roar, the two booking agents suddenly bolted off to a little distance, and the crowd shouldered them instantly to a greater distance still. The whole mob began to cheer.

"Barney Dwyer's no cheapskate!" yelled one cowpuncher.

And they all cheered again, tumultuously.

Barney was glad of that cheering. He would have been gladder still to escape from them all, but he could not manage that while the mob was shouldering about him, and the red mare was unable to run. So he leaned and laid his grasp on the round of iron that encircled her leg.

It was an ordinary horseshoe the toes of which had been hammered in to make the ring complete and enclose the slender cannon bone of the mare's near foreleg.

"Now we're gonna see!" exclaimed a big fellow with the soot of the blacksmith shop still on his forearms and with a swipe of it across his forehead. "Now we're gonna see, and now we're gonna be able to tell what liars some folks is that say that they seen him *break* a horseshoe."

Barney already had his grip inside the heavy iron ring, and he tugged at the iron circle. The flesh of his fingers brushed against the bone vainly, until he heard the blacksmith's remark, and when he perceived that there was a silly trickery about the whole thing, and that this had been devised as a test for his strength, a fury boiled up in Barney Dwyer. He jerked. If that band were of iron, his hands and wrists became of steel, and unbent it enough to draw it free from the leg entirely.

He faced the blacksmith and hurled the unbent shoe down into the dust before him. Barney Dwyer was utterly mindless of the shout of joyous astonishment, and of the long, amazed face of the blacksmith.

"It's all right to make a fool of me," exclaimed Barney, "but if you touch my horse again, I'll see what *your* bones are made of!"

The big blacksmith said not a word. He merely bent and picked up the unbent horseshoe from the dust at his feet, and then slunk away through the crowd.

Barney swung on high into the saddle. They

scattered back before him. He was about to ride off when a tall fellow with an authoritative air came out from the side of the lane, where he had been watching critically. He had just suppressed a smile of satisfaction, and now he said: "Dwyer, I'm Parmelee of the Parmelee Ranch. Will you talk business with me?"

Barney instantly jumped down to the ground. There were scores of witnesses of the conversation that followed.

"Yes, Mister Parmelee?" said Barney.

"You know my ranch?" asked Robert Parmelee.

"No, sir," Barney said respectfully.

"It's up yonder," said Parmelee. "Up there in the pass. Up there in the hole-in-the-wall country. D'you see?" He pointed toward the ragged, distant tide of the mountains.

"I see," said Barney.

"I need a foreman to take charge for me," said Parmelee. "Will you take the job? It's not fifteen hundred dollars a week. It's not more than a hundred and fifty a month . . . to start with."

Barney glanced hastily around him, and flushed. He wished that he might be alone with Parmelee to make the confession that followed. But the truth had to out. It was impossible for him to lie, or to allow false ideas to be afloat about him.

Then he said, confronting the lean, shrewd face of Parmelee: "The fact is that I'm not fit to boss a gang, Mister Parmelee. I'm not a very good hand with a rope. And I don't know how to handle cattle very well. I couldn't take such a responsibility as running your ranch for you."

At this, a little hush fell over the crowd. They knew Parmelee. A good many of them had eloquent reasons for knowing him. He himself grinned sourly.

"I'll run my own ranch and handle my own cows," he said. "But the men I need up there are men made of iron. And I see that you're a fellow who can *bend* iron. That's the fellow I want for a foreman. I have plenty of acres of grasslands. I have plenty of dirty rustlers for neighbors, too. I want 'punchers made of iron. I want 'punchers that Winchester bullets will bounce off. And I want a foreman that's able to bend those iron men. Dwyer, don't tell me whether or not you're the right man. Just tell me that you'll do your best."

"I'll do my best," said Barney, staring. He was like a child forced to answer a teacher.

"Then come up there tomorrow. I'll be waiting for you," said Parmelee.

With that, he turned his back, abruptly, and was gone.

III

It was later in that day when Harris Fielding, lawyer extraordinary, talked with his two clients in the Coffeeville jail. Adler and McGregor stood on one side of the steel grating, and little Harris Fielding walked impatiently up and down on the outer side of it. The guard stood in a far corner, only making sure that the visitor made no effort to pass anything into the hands of the accused men. It was an old frame building, that jail, as has been said, and yet it had an excellent reputation, for the cells were of the best bars of tool-proof steel, and the sheriff saw to it that the guards were of the best sort of fighting material.

Harris Fielding was terse and excited. As he walked up and down, he talked only while he was pacing in one direction. As he moved in the other, he silently fixed his glance on the long white face, the white hair, the black eyes of Doc Adler—eyes that were perennially young, for evil was in him like a bright fountain of youth. Doc Adler sat in a chair, his head thrust forward by the crook in his back, while McGregor stood beside him, resting a hand on the back of the chair. McGregor did the talking, his face, hard as iron, never changing its expression no matter what he said.

149

"I've got good news and bad news," said Harris Fielding.

"At the price we pay you, you ought to have nothing but good news," said McGregor.

"You think I can pull a man clear when he's all in hell except one fingertip?" snapped Harris Fielding, shaking a bony finger at McGregor. Fuming cigarettes had stained that finger yellow; his complexion was almost the same hue.

"You've done it before," said McGregor. "And you can do it again. What's the good news?"

"Big Barney Dwyer refuses to press the case against you. He won't go into the courtroom and give testimony against you," said Harris Fielding.

Adler lifted his head like an old buzzard on a roost, smelling food. McGregor's lip curled.

"He thinks that he can make us forget other things he's done, eh? He's turning yellow, is he?" said McGregor.

"I'm telling you the facts, not the motives," answered Harris Fielding. "But from what the people say, there's no fear in him. Now for my bad news, and it's enough to overweigh the good news. Your man, Justis, the big fellow with the long black hair, is ready to turn state's evidence."

"Justis?" said McGregor calmly. "Then get to him, and stop him."

"I've got to him," said Harris Fielding. "I didn't need to wait for orders to do that. I got to him, but I can't stop him."

"Money will stop him. Money will choke him . . . the traitor!" said McGregor.

"Money won't stop him. I offered him fifty thousand dollars to keep his mouth shut. He won't take a penny. He's sick of you, he says, ever since Adler put a bullet through the shoulder of the girl. He says that a man who would shoot a woman isn't fit for murder, even. Adler did it, though. And Adler was your right-hand man. So Justis is through with you."

"I've put money by the tens of thousands in the hands of Justis," remarked McGregor, "and now he turns on me, the snake!"

"He says that you and Adler are a disgrace to the West," said Harris Fielding. "He says that burning is what you ought to have, and not hanging. He says that he'd like to light the fire that roasts you."

McGregor looked down at Adler, and Adler looked up at McGregor.

"When I'm out of this," said McGregor, "I'll call on Mister Justis even before I call on Barney Dwyer."

"Boys," said Harris Fielding, pausing at last in his pacing, and standing directly before the pair, "I don't think that you're going to get out."

"We're going to get out. I have some things to do, before I die," answered McGregor. "What's the idea, Fielding? Trying to shake us down for a bigger retainer?"

"If I can't do more than I've managed, up to this point," answered Fielding, "I'll give back the retainer. I'm not trying to shake you down. I'm just telling you how near the rope you are."

"You don't see a way to save us? What about the judge? You said that you knew him."

"I do. And he's as crooked as a dog's hind leg. But when I talked to him last night, he said that there's nothing that he dares to try when the trial takes place. He says that the whole district around here thinks that Barney Dwyer is a hero."

"Hero? He's a half-wit," said McGregor.

"He may be a little simple about some things," answered Fielding. "He may be too trusting and good-natured, but I should say that he's something more than a half-wit. At least, he's beaten you and Adler . . . the wisest crooks in the whole range. He's beaten you over and over."

With one voice, both Adler and McGregor croaked: "Luck! He had some crazy luck. Beginners' luck. He couldn't sit in with us through the whole game. We'd have his scalp," added McGregor.

"Maybe you would. I hear you say so," said Harris Fielding. "But just now he's riding on top. The men around here begin to wear their hats like Barney Dwyer . . . a little on the back of their heads. The boys and the youngsters try to walk like him, slowly. Everyone tries to talk like him, slowly. Everyone is quieter. Just because he's refused to testify against you, because he doesn't want even the blood of his enemies on his hands, these mountaineers worship him. Today, I heard a man say . . . 'As true as Barney Dwyer.' He's a proverb for everything honest and straight and simple and true. The decent men in this town won't speak to me, simply because they know that I'm your hired lawyer. No wonder the judge says that he wouldn't dare to favor you. He'd be lynched. And any juryman who failed to find you guilty would be lynched, too . . . and *pronto*. Maybe I paint a black picture for you, but it's a true one. If you stand your trial in Coffeeville, you're a pair of dead ones."

McGregor closed his eyes and grew slightly pale.

Adler remarked: "Well, now that we know the rock bottom, we can start building."

"Building on what?" snapped McGregor.

"Building to get out of this place . . . this jail. If staying on here means hanging, then we gotta leave."

"How'll you get out?" asked Harris Fielding.

"With our brains," said Adler.

"Burn your brains!" growled Fielding, and walked straight out of the jail.

He went to the hotel, packed his bag, and paid his bill.

"I wash my hands of the Adler-McGregor case," said Harris Fielding. And he went to the railroad station, stepping out briskly in his natty suit of grey tweed. "They're as guilty as hell . . . and that's why I'm washing my hands of the case," said Harris Fielding unprofessionally.

As a matter of fact, he thought that the pair were little better than dead men.

An hour later, big long-haired Justis had sworn out the statement by which he saved his own neck, and put that of McGregor into the halter. It was an economical statement. As for Adler, it could be proved that he had fired a bullet at a woman with intent to kill. That would be enough to settle him in a Western law court. As for McGregor, the statement of Justis cooked him. It proved very simply and with concrete evidence that it was not young Leonard Peary who had shot and killed Buddy Marsh, driver of the Coffeeville Stage to Timberline. Instead, Peary was cleared of the murder and the blame was placed squarely on the shoulders of McGregor.

The district attorney was very contented, after he had that statement in his hands. Coffeeville was contented, too.

But in their adjoining cells at the jail, that evening, hope was not dead in the breasts of McGregor and Adler. Like a strange harbinger of better fortune, there arrived a visitor to call upon McGregor, and he was permitted to chat with the captive for a moment, standing in front of the bars of the cell. For everyone knew that this was

Wash, the old Negro, dusty gray with age, who for years had been the servant to McGregor, and before him to the honorable family from which McGregor descended.

So the jailor let in Wash, and stood only near enough to see that nothing was passed from hand to hand.

Old Wash, his hat in his hand, his head bowed, stood in the aisle in front of his master's cell and let the tears, unregarded, roll down his face.

Adler sat with his buzzard face pressed close against the bars, watching, listening. Like a bird, he said nothing. Like a bird his eyes were sharp as polished beads.

But the voice of McGregor went on softly, smoothly, saying: "Wash, did you bring down the bunch of skeleton keys and pass keys?"

"Yes, sir," said Wash.

"Take those keys out to the edge of the town, up the creek, tonight, as soon as it's dark. There's a grove of poplar trees, yonder. Take the keys there. And have two good horses there. And wait."

"Yes, sir," said Wash.

"I may not come tonight, or tomorrow night. But have the keys and the horses there. Have them there every night. Every night until they hang me by the neck."

"Yes, sir," said Wash.

"Have you brought plenty of money, Wash?"

"Ten thousand dollars, sir."

"That ought to be enough. Get the finest horses that you can buy. Have rifles and revolvers. Everything that I might need. You understand?"

"Yes sir," said Wash.

"And if I hang, Wash," went on McGregor, "all of that money is yours. That and everything else you can put your hands on. You know where to find it, too."

"Old Wash ain't gonna need money, if you come to an end, sir," said the Negro.

"Don't talk rot," said McGregor. "You'll live twenty years more. Now get out of here and do what I tell you."

So Wash left the jail, and presently afterward the head jailor went his final rounds for the night, and lingered to shine his lantern on the manacles that bound the hands of McGregor and Adler. He nodded, satisfied, and moved on his way. The jail settled into darkness broken only by the glow of a single smoky lantern toward the center of the cell room. Other men began to snore, but Adler and McGregor were talking in small whispers, bending their minds on the problem of life or of death.

IV

"Fielding has run out on us," said McGregor.

"It's a sinkin' ship when that rat leaves it," commented Adler.

"Burn our brains," muttered McGregor. "He told us to burn our brains to get us out of here."

"We'll burn 'em, then," said Adler. "There ain't a tight place in the world that thinkin' won't make wide enough for a horse and man to ride out of safe and sound."

"Ride us out of here, then, Doc," said McGregor.

"Burn our brains, eh?" muttered Adler. "Burn our brains."

"There's twenty chinks and crannies right through the crazy old walls of the jail," said McGregor.

"It ain't the walls, it's the steel bars inside of 'em that count," said Adler. "It's a funny thing, Mack. Here's me, that's beat the law all of these years, and yet it comes and grabs me right at the end of my life. It's like a story book. I went and beat it all of these years. And I put my brains up ag'in' some of the smartest that ever stepped. And always I beat 'em, till I come up ag'in' this Barney Dwyer."

"The half-wit!" snarled McGregor.

"Well, if he had a whole wit, God help you and me and crooks like us," answered Adler. "Don't talk down about him, Mack. Because if you make him small, you make us mighty tiny. He beat us. He beat us both. We was settin' on top of the heap. These here mountains knew us like sheep know a pair of old bellwethers. But still he beat us both . . . him and him alone."

"Luck is the difference," said McGregor.

"Burn our brains to get out . . . burn our brains," murmured Adler. "And even Harris Fielding has gone and left us. He wouldn't leave while there was a ghost of a hope, son. That ain't his way. I recollect Pudge Davis, that killed the three brothers down there in Phoenix. They got him dead to rights. But he found Harris Fielding for a lawyer, and Fielding sets him free. You recollect how he done that?"

"No. I don't remember. How?"

"There was an eyewitness that seen the three killings, all in a row. He swore to everything. He even got down to a point where Fielding just seemed helpless, and kept askin' simple, foolish questions, like he was just tryin' to fill up time and *pretend* to do his best for his client. And then he asked among other questions, the color of the necktie that Pudge Davis was wearin' the day he done the murders, and, by jiminy, the witness told him that, too, and told him the pattern of it, too. And right then, Harris Fielding, he clapped a hand over his own necktie and bellers out and says . . . 'Tell me the color of my necktie will you? I've been wearing the same one every day of the trial' . . . which was a lie . . . 'and now you tell me the color of my necktie.' And the witness, he couldn't do it. He only guessed, and he guessed wrong. And when it come to talkin' to the jury, Harris Fielding, he talked about nothin' else but that . . . about what a sneakin' liar that witness was and how all of his story had oughta be throwed out. And by the leapin' thunder, they *did* throw it out. They made Pudge Davis a free man. And he lived a whole six months after that, till a greaser knifed him one day in Mexico City, about a gal. A yaller gal. But Fielding got him free. And only took twenty-five hundred dollars away from him, which was all that he had. Yes, sir, it's pretty wonderful what a gent can do that's a smart lawyer. But even while Fielding knew that he could get a *hundred* thousand out of us, he didn't try. He threw up the sponge. He quit."

"Damn him," said McGregor. "And damn you too, Adler. I don't want to think about how other folks got out of jail. I want to think about our own case. If we could get some good saws in here. . . ."

"There'd make a terrible screechin' on the tool-proof steel," said Adler. "And there's gents on guard here night and day, always watchin' and waitin' for a whisper out of our cells."

"We've got to think," insisted McGregor.

"Never crowd your brain, son," said Doc Adler. "Never put a whip on your brain. A gent's mind is a free worker, till it's crowded. Take when you try to remember a name that's skipped your memory. You try hard. You force. You crowd on steam. And the dog-gone' mind lays right down on you like a balky horse, and don't do nothing. But suppose that you quit tryin', and just whistle a tune, and make yourself a cigarette, and right away that name pops up in your mind, easy as nothin' at all."

"All right," said McGregor. "But every night that passes brings us a night nearer to hell. They'll put us on trial, tomorrow."

"Burn our minds, eh?" said Doc Adler. "Burn our minds to get away? No, but by God, we might burn the jail."

"Rather die in a fire than by a rope?" asked McGregor.

"I've got the head of a match in the pocket of this coat," said Adler. "And the wood of this here wall is dry as tinder. And there's an old newspaper in my cell. By thunder, Mack, it's the right idea."

"They take us out because the damn' jail begins to burn? Is that it?"

"That's it," said Adler. "Anyway, we'll see."

Presently faint sounds of the rustling of paper came from his cell. After that, there was the crackling noise of a match being struck—a most illegal act in that tinder box of a building. And immediately afterward, the thick, sweet smoke of burning paper poured out of the cell of Adler.

Neither he nor McGregor uttered a sound. The flames that rose from the paper made a soft fluttering sound. Dull waves of light were thrown out from the cell. But the other prisoners slept soundly, and the guards gave no token. Into the noise of the burning of the paper came another sound, the sharp, resinous crackling as the dry pine boards that composed the wall of the jail began to catch from the heat.

The moment that they were fairly ignited, a gust of wind took the fire rushing and snapping up the outer wall of the jail. A man yelled loudly from the street. And as a gust of heat swept through the jail itself, other prisoners wakened and began to screech.

"Fire! Fire!"

There was a trampling of feet. The guards came running. Water was brought. The whole floor of the jail was soon awash with it, but that did not master the flames that were running to the apex of the roof by this time.

The jailor came and shook his fist through the bars at Adler. "You did this, damn you. I've a mind to leave you there, to roast!" he yelled.

But already the doors of the cells were being unlocked and the prisoners turned loose. Adler and McGregor among the rest were herded into the street in front of the flaming building. The townspeople were gathering. And high above them the flames disappeared in flinging armfuls that threw brief waves of light over all the town, and made the creek run like a stream of gold through Coffeeville.

There were twenty of those prisoners, most of them in for nothing more than vagrancy. And there were only four guards. They picked out the chief prisoners, however. The head jailor himself took charge of big McGregor. And his next best man was with old Doc Adler. Yet giving so little heed to his charge that he merely kept a firm grip on Adler's arm and watched the flames of the burning jail, while Doc Adler whispered to the tramps nearby: "Now, boys, one rush and we're all as free as the day we were born. All together, and one good rush, and we'll kick their coppers in the face, and slide out of Coffeeville while the rest of the town is still throwin' water to keep the whole town from burnin' up."

From far and near, as the flames from the jail shot high in the air and great showers of sparks descended over the town, men could be seen on roof tops, little black forms against the sky, hauling up buckets of water from the ground and wetting down the shingles.

There were surprisingly few, except women and children, left to watch the conflagration.

And the little herd of prisoners, closely compacted by the guards who watched over them, began to stir a little. A muttering came up from them, just as a moaning sound will come up from a herd that is bedded down in uneasy weather. And as a herd will start into a stampede when a single cow leaps to its feet and rushes off, so the whole gang of the prisoners got into sudden motion when a huge Negro in the center of the bunch bounded high into the air and yelled: "Boys, I'm goin'!"

There was one instant of wavering. Then the whole crowd lurched straight forward.

The guards were brave men and knew their business. But they were kicked to the ground, or beaten down with the blows delivered by manacled wrists, and the whole mass of the prisoners swept off up the street.

At the very next lane, two figures detached from the rest and slipped down to the edge of the creek. Stealthily they worked back up the side of the water until they came to a small grove of trees and into that they disappeared.

Behind them, the jail was already rotting to the ground in a welter of flames, leaving the red hot skeleton of the cells still standing, unharmed.

V

To Barney, all the news of that escape was lacking. He had left Coffeeville in the afternoon, with his roll of belongings strapped behind his saddle, a Winchester thrust into the saddle holster under his knee, and a heavy Colt revolver. He merely paused at the house of Dr. Swain to see Susan Jones.

It was a hot afternoon, and the doctor and his wife had carried the girl into the shade of the house, in the garden. There she lay propped with pillows on a small camp cot, when Barney came to her. Mrs. Swain promptly got up from the chair where she had been sitting to read to the girl and offered that seat to Barney, but he could not disturb her comfort. It hardly even occurred to him that it might be better if he were alone with Sue Jones. He wanted to be near her, to touch her hand, to look closely into her face, and, for that purpose, he dropped on one knee beside the cot.

The girl's face was an almost even white when he came. It turned at once to an almost even red. She bit her lip. She was ashamed of Barney for not having sufficient understanding to see that they should be alone. She was ashamed of herself for not appreciating more his calm lack of self-consciousness.

"You stay, Missus Swain," she said. "It's all right. Do stay."

Mrs. Swain remained, but uneasily.

And Barney said: "You're better, Sue. Your eye is clearer."

"I'm better," said the girl.

He took her hand with a wonderful gentleness.

"There's a Mister Robert Parmelee who offered me a place today on his ranch, to act as foreman, at a hundred and fifty dollars a month. I told him that I really don't know enough to handle the cattle. He says that doesn't matter. He thinks, for some reason, that I may be able to handle the sort of men that he needs to have on his place. I've told him that I'd come . . . if you permit it, Sue."

The girl blushed more deeply.

"If you decided to go, of course you're the master of yourself, Barney," she said.

"But you know," said Barney, looking at her in surprise, "that all of your ideas are sure to be better than mine. I wouldn't dream of going without your permission, Sue. Why does it anger you for me to say that? Why do you look at Missus Swain?"

The anger of Sue Jones seemed to grow every moment, until she was positively glaring at Barney.

Mrs. Swain, who felt more and more uncomfortable, was drawn to leave at once, and yet her curiosity was so fascinated that she could not help remaining. For this was the hero, the man who was so worshipped and feared through all the length of the range. This was the fellow who had quelled the great McGregor and all his men. And yet now he was as gentle and simple as a child, before this girl. Furthermore, it was clear that this very simplicity was a little more than Sue Jones liked to see exhibited in public.

Mrs. Swain said: "My dear Mister Dwyer, of course you know what sort of a place the Parmelee Ranch is?"

"He said that it was up there in the mountains, and that the country was rough," said Barney. "He said that he needed rough men, too. He thought, somehow, that I could be useful in working with them."

"No one but a Robert Parmelee," said Mrs. Swain, "would ever have attempted to use such land. He got it for a song. But he spent money on cattle to stock it. They increased for a time. People even thought that he might win in the end . . . but now matters go from bad to worse, and I hear they're running off the cows a great deal faster than he can raise 'em."

"Who are runnin' them off?" asked the girl.

"The squatters who are all over the mountains, there. They each have a patch of land, and they do a little farming, a little trapping, hunting, fishing, and sometimes they work by the day in the big lumber camps. But they're a rough lot, and they don't see any difference between wild deer and half wild range cattle. You see? They don't think that it's stealing when they run off with a few cows. They kill, cure the meat, and tan the hides. And when they've done that, they haven't a care on their consciences. The sheriffs have tried their hands at bringing in law and order, but how can law and order get on when several hundred people all feel the same way about anything? Dear Mister Dwyer, it's simply a catch. Of course you can't handle those men. Nobody could. Robert Parmelee is a dry soul, and I suppose that he was simply laughing at you up his sleeve. He's about to move his cows away from that part of the world. I understand that he's already trying to buy land in Texas."

Barney listened attentively to this tale. But in the end, he seemed to feel no conviction about what he had heard.

He merely said to the girl: "Well, Sue, should I go or stay?"

She seemed to be more irritated than ever, by this question, and she exclaimed: "Barney, how can I tell? Do you think that you're strong enough to handle several hundred wild people? I've heard about the rustlers and the squatters up there in the mountains. Everybody has. And what could you do with them, being only one man?"

"I don't know," said Barney. "Maybe I could do nothing, and maybe, on the other hand, I could manage to help. It seems too bad, Sue, that honest people can't make their way against thieves. Don't you think that it's too bad?"

"Yes," the girl said faintly, staring at him. "I suppose that it *is* too bad. Are you going to try to reform the whole world, Barney?"

"Oh, no," said Barney naïvely. "I wouldn't try to do any such important thing. I only want to do what's right, when I'm told to do it and when it seems clear. If Mister Parmelee is in trouble . . . why shouldn't I go to work for him? And you know, Sue, that I have to be making a little money before we can be married."

Mrs. Swain ducked her head and frowned in order to cover her smile. But Sue Jones saw the smile, nevertheless.

"It's true," she said. "And then . . . there's another thing. You have to be your own manager, Barney. You have to be able to make your own decisions before you can take care of a family, I suppose?"

"Do I?" said Barney, opened-eyed. "I didn't know that. I thought that you would always make all the decisions. I thought that wives always did, in happy homes."

Mrs. Swain laughed outright at this, and Sue grew pinker than ever.

"And what do the husbands do, Mister Dwyer?" asked the doctor's wife. "What do you understand the husbands do?"

"Why," said Barney simply, "I suppose that the husbands work very hard and bring home their money every Saturday."

The two women looked at one another and both laughed this time.

"But don't go to the Parmelee place," said Mrs. Swain.

He looked at the girl. "Shall I not, Sue?" he asked.

"Yes, yes. Go," said Susan Jones. "Be your own master. Go your own way."

"But you're not angry, Sue?" he asked her, terribly concerned.

"No," said the girl.

"And if I go, you'll follow me when you're well, Sue, on the way that I take?"

"Yes," she said, blushing hotly once more.

He leaned over her. "Will you kiss me good bye, Sue?" he said.

She pursed her lips, silently, and so he touched them, stood up, bade Mrs. Swain good bye, and went out to the red mare that waited at the gate. He swung into the saddle, waved his hat in a happy farewell, and was gone.

The sound of the hoof beats still swung back to them when the doctor's wife murmured: "Why are you ashamed, Sue? Tell me that."

The girl closed her eyes tightly and made a gesture with the arm that was not bandaged. "Because," she exclaimed, "sometimes I think that the gossips are right, and that he has only half of his wits about him . . . and then at other times I feel that he's just a great, simple-hearted hero, without malice or meanness or sharpness."

Mrs. Swain narrowed her eyes a little, and stopped smiling. "I understand," she said. "But I'll tell you something. If he's a fool, he must be a very great one, because he's done some very great things."

The girl nodded, and sighed. "And I've seen some of them," she confessed. "I've seen him always fearless, always gentle, always true. And yet, Missus Swain . . . sometimes I wish . . . sometimes I wish that he were a little less good, and a little more clever."

"Good men are always a little simple," said Mrs. Swain. "And especially good husbands."

She said this with a great deal of emphasis, and the two women found something between them that made them smile silently at one another.

VI

But if Barney Dwyer showed no appreciation of the shadow that had crossed the mind of the girl, he felt it all the more keenly. He did not know why she was unhappy, but was sure that it was his fault. He was sure that she had been more than a little ashamed of him. And as he rode the red mare up through the hills toward the Parmelee Ranch, he sighed more than once. He looked up with a frown of resolution toward the sky, telling himself that he must gather his strength again, and more mightily than ever, if he were to make Sue Jones really his.

He was used to pain. He was used to contempt. The sudden air of adulation that surrounded him made him less happy than uneasy. He was not accustomed to such an atmosphere. His very strength had made him more often cursed than blessed for the pitchforks and the spades that he broke, until, finally, he had matched that strength against McGregor and that band of cut-throats in the mountains. His reward had been fame and popularity. His greatest reward of all had been the promise of the girl to marry him. But as he called up her picture and dwelt again on the memory of that pretty brown face, so brown that the eyes seemed doubly blue in it, he told himself over and over that she was much too good for him. He would have to labor with all his might to hold her, after she had been won.

And, somehow, if he could put out his hands on the problem that troubled Parmelee, if he could make a safe and respected home for them even among the dangers of those mountains, would not Sue regain her respect and her affection for him?

That was the reason Barney sighed as he

journeyed along. And yet he was purely happy, in a sense. He was happy because he was alone with the red bay mare, and though she had no words, yet she supplied him with a sort of conversation that he could understand. The lifting of her head, the pricking of her ears, and the very way she paused on a hilltop to look down into the hollow beneath, as though she were prepared for anything in the world, gave a thrill to the heart of Barney Dwyer.

As they came to the steeper inclines, he dismounted as usual, and went on foot, and he was still on foot when he came with the evening of the day to the pass, and in the darkness he reached the ranch house. It was merely a long, low shed, with a barn behind it. He pushed open the door to inquire at the house: "Is this the Parmelee place?" And there he saw a big table with six men seated at it, and one of the six was Robert Parmelee.

The rancher did not rise. He merely said: "Put your horse up, and come in for supper."

So Barney put up the horse. He found the feed box, gave the mare a feed of crushed barley, and came back to the house. The pump stood outside the building, with several wash basins of graniteware leaning against the base of it. He pumped one of those basins full, found a wedge of yellow laundry soap, and scrubbed himself thoroughly.

When he had dried his face and hands, he stood for a moment to breathe more deeply of the purity of the thin mountain air, of which lungs can drink forever and ever and never reach satiety. Then he looked upward at the black outlines of the summits, and finally went into the house.

There was one lamp with a round burner to give light, and it showed him a rough, tattered set of ranch hands. They had finished eating. They sat about smoking Bull Durham tobacco wrapped in filmy tissues of wheat-straw paper. Silently they sat, staring at the remnants of soggy cold potatoes boiled in their wrappers that remained in the dish in the center of the table, and the few scraps of beefsteak that remained on a platter in the midst of a sea of white, congealed grease.

The potato dish and the platter of meat were shoved toward him. A Negro cook came in with a plate and knife and fork and spoon and tin cup, which were rattled down in front of him, and so Barney fell to work.

He felt hard, keen eyes fastened upon him with indifference. Only Bob Parmelee seemed to be paying no attention, until, after a moment, the men began to push back their chairs.

Then Parmelee said: "Wait a minute, boys. This is your new straw boss. This is the new foreman."

"More new than foreman, he looks to me," said one of the men insolently, and stalked out of the room. The others laughed. The braying noise of their laughter grated upon the ears of Barney, and he heard the door slam behind them as they issued from the dining room into the darkness.

"Tough, eh?" said Parmelee.

Barney nodded, frowning.

"You'll have to lick 'em into shape," said Parmelee. "I told 'em that you were the new boss. I didn't tell them the name of the boss. That might make an impression, but impressions don't last long up here, the weather's too changeable. A lot too changeable. A man has to make a new reputation up here, every day of his life. Understand?"

"Yes," Barney said miserably.

"These fellows are a tough lot. Nobody but tough *hombres* would stay for even a day, up here on my ranch. There are too many bullets in the air to suit most. These fellows have nerve, and they know their business. But they don't see any reason for doing their work well when there's nothing to show for it. The cows they take care of are off under their noses, and they can't do anything about it."

Barney nodded. His heart was growing smaller and colder.

"When the morning comes," said Parmelee, "you've got to start in. You've got to show the crowd that you're the boss. After you've shown them that, you've got to start to work to get back some of the stolen cattle. A good fifty two-year-old dogies were run off today. We happen to know that, because the fifty were all pooled in a bit of good pasture down in the flat by the creek, and Brick counted 'em this morning. This evening, they're gone."

"Couldn't they be tracked?" asked Barney.

"They were tracked, all right. They were tracked right onto the Washburn place. Old Washburn and his boys have those dogies, now, as sure as I'm alive. I know it. The boys know it. But what can we do about it?"

"Do?" Barney said, amazed. "Why, you could go and ask for them, I should think."

Parmelee's chair screeched as he jumped to his feet. "*Ask* for them?" he shouted. "You think that *asking* would get them back?"

And with that, without even saying good night, he stalked from the room.

Barney knew, somehow, that his employer would not return to bid him good night, or to point out the bunks. He sat gloomily over his coffee until it was cold. Then, leaving it half drunk, he got up from the table and went out to the barn. There he leaned on the manger and patted the shoulder of the red mare, for a time. She could know, beyond doubt, if horses have memory, of far worse times than these, through which they nevertheless had lived together.

He felt comforted, and went back to the house. Half of it was evidently given up to the kitchen

175

and the dining room, and the other half must be for the bunks, so he pushed open the door at the end of the house, and was promptly covered with a deluge of cold water. The bucket in which it had been balanced on top of the half-closed door crashed right over his head and fitted down on his shoulders like a man's hat on the head of a child.

And six men sat up in their bunks to shout with laughter and with joy at the spectacle he presented in the light of the single lantern. Someone turned up the light so that he could be seen the better.

That bawling laughter, those brutal faces, those bestial, gleaming eyes, were all familiar to him. He had always been the butt of all the practical jokes.

So he said nothing, uttered not a word of complaint, but, taking the bucket from his head and shoulders, he strove to smile—a very faint appreciation of whatever humor might be concealed in this jest.

And this smiling brought an increase, only, in the noise. He saw Bob Parmelee laughing even more loudly than the rest, and this amazed him. In Parmelee, at least, he felt that he should have been able to find a friend.

He put his bedroll aside, stripped off his clothes, wrung them out dry, and came back naked to find a bunk.

"Look at Fatty," said an obscure voice.

For the body of Barney Dwyer was as sleek as the body of a seal, and how were these observers to know that it was not fat but fine muscle that was packed away under the pink of his skin?

"That fat'll burn up, like a lamp burns up oil," said another.

And again came the ominous chuckle. "Straw boss, straw hell," said another.

This brought noisier mirth, again.

There were a double double-deck bunks around the length and width of the room. Half of these were occupied already. The other lower bunks were heaped with odds and ends of possessions of the various hands.

Barney approached one bunk on which was heaped merely a number of old magazines and newspapers, and he started to remove this litter to make place for his roll. But promptly a red-headed fellow sat up, across the room, and bawled out: "Leave them things be! Some of them magazines is mine! Whatcha mean, mixin' everything up? Who are you, anyway?"

Barney said nothing. He replaced what he had disturbed.

"Don't be so dog-gone' hard on the poor kid, Red," advised someone.

"Kid be damned. He's the boss, ain't he?" asked Red.

"Boss my foot," said another.

And again they laughed loudly.

They laughed still more, in an ecstasy of derision, as they saw Barney patiently making down his bedding roll on an upper bunk. But he was merely saying to himself that it was an old, old story. As for many years before, again he would become the butt and the laughingstock of the cowpunchers. Why had Parmelee dreamed that he, Barney Dwyer, could handle these fellows?

His wretchedness of mind, his sinking of the heart, kept him awake for a long time. He seemed, as in the old days, once more to be walled away from his fellow men.

At last he slept, and, wakening in the morning, he heard the cook already calling, through the half light of the dawn: "Come and get it! Come and get it!"

He tumbled out with the rest, and went to wash, but as he began to pump a wash basin full, outside the kitchen door, the loud, ranting voice of Red shouted: "Leave that wash basin alone! That's my wash basin!"

Obediently Barney put it down.

He had to wait until the others had finished their ablutions before he could wash in turn. And by the time he was ready for it, the long roller towel of coarse cotton cloth was soggy with moisture and dark with grime.

When he came into the dining room, someone

sang out: "Stand up, boys. Here comes the boss!"

And a roar of laughter greeted this bright sally.

He sat down.

"Ain't that your chair, Red?" asked a voice.

They roared again, and Red most of all. He was a powerful fellow in his early twenties, with a flaring shock of uncontrollable red hair, freckles across his nose, and a great blunt jaw, and pale, berserker eyes that continually craved trouble.

That miserable meal ended, finally, and Barney stood up among the last. There was only Parmelee in the room, as he turned toward the door.

"One minute," said Parmelee. "I dunno what you have up your sleeve, Dwyer. I can't imagine what. But I know that you're making a fool of yourself."

"I don't know what to do," Barney said sadly.

"Break one of them in two. That's the thing to do," said Parmelee.

"I don't like fighting," said Barney truthfully, and gently.

"You . . . don't like . . . fighting?" echoed Parmelee, raging. "And what the devil did I bring you up here for? A Sunday school teacher? A hundred and fifty dollars a month for teaching the boys hymns, perhaps? You get on the job and whip this gang into shape before night, or you're fired, Dwyer, and be damned to you!"

179

VII

Wretchedly Barney dragged himself out to the barn, for the body is heavy when the spirit is weak. He saddled and bridled the mare and took her out to the watering trough. He saw the keen eyes of the others fastened upon him.

"Where'd you steal that horse, boy?" asked Red. "Or did your pa give her to you? That horse is meant for a man."

Barney swallowed the insult with a gulp. "I only wanted to ask you men," said Barney, "if one of you would show me the way to the Washburn place. Will you?"

"If one of us would show you the way to the Washburn place," mimicked Red, "what would you do when you got there? Get a licking?"

"I want to ask them to drive back the cattle they took away yesterday," said Barney.

They stood at the heads of their horses, staring, thunderstruck. Then, led by Red, they burst into whooping peals of mirth.

"He's gonna go and *ask* the Washburns for them dogies. He's a half-wit!" shouted Red.

The stern, quick voice of Parmelee said: "Phil, show him the way to the Washburns. And stay close enough to see whether he has the nerve to ride up to the house."

That was how Barney found himself on the way through the ragged hills of the pass until, before him, he saw a sprawling shack like that of Parmelee, only much smaller. It was a scant two miles from the ranch, tucked back in a little valley where a scrap of plow land stood black beside a creek, and some sheep grazed behind a log fence.

At a break in the trees, Phil said: "All right . . . boss. There's the Washburn house. And them are the Washburns, settin' around the table, outside of the house. Lemme see you go up and brace 'em. If they don't kick you off your horse and clean over the divide, I'll eat my hat, Fatty."

Barney rode on. There were four men seated around what appeared to be a table with a rounded, irregular top, at a distance, but, coming nearer, he saw that it was simply a great boulder, with jags and knobs projecting from the side, and the top spreading out like the head of a mushroom. Around that table, eating their breakfast, appeared the Washburns. The father was gray-headed and gray-bearded. Otherwise, they were hard to tell one from the other, for all were bearded, all were mustached, all were huge fellows in dirt-blackened patched flannel shirts. A slatternly woman went back and forth through the doorway of the house, serving her menfolk.

No one stood up when Barney came near and dismounted. But eating was suspended for an instant while bright, savage eyes glared at the stranger.

Barney saw that he had come so far out on the rim of the world that even hospitality was forgotten here.

"Who are you?" asked the father. "There ain't any hand-outs for bums on my ranch."

"I'm from the Parmelee Ranch," said Barney. "It seems that Mister Parmelee feels that some cattle . . . fifty of 'em . . . took the wrong way across the hills, and may have gone close to your place. He wants to know if you've seen them?"

Through a blank moment of silence, they stared. Then, of one mind, the five men arose from the table and faced Barney. At the door of the house, against the blackness of the interior, Barney saw the woman standing to watch, with a toothless grin.

Said the father: "If Parmelee thinks that something of his is over here on my place, what in hell does he mean by sendin' one fat-faced fool to get it?"

Barney was stunned. He had expected discourtesy, but not this degree of it. He had hardly known what he would do when his request was refused, but he had felt that the moment would come when his back would be against the wall. For the sake of his job, for the sake of his entire future, for the sake of his hopes of happiness with Sue, he would have to manage something on the spur of the moment. And that spur was now entering his side.

The father walked slowly toward him. The four huge sons advanced, spreading out a little to either side. It was like the stalking of five great wolves.

"I'll tell you what I'll do," said the elder Washburn. "I'll send fifty cows to Parmelee . . . the damned land grabber . . . when that there rock is tore up from the ground and rolled down the hill into the creek. I'll . . ."

"All right," said Barney. "Let me try the rock." He was glad of it. No matter for the failure. If it were a problem on which he could set the strength of his hands, he felt that he would be in heaven. As for the irony in the speech of the elder Washburn, he was not even aware of it. So he stepped past the puzzled faces of those big men and laid his grip on the lower ledge of the mushroom-shaped rock. Then he lifted.

Such strength as his could not easily be unlocked and bestowed like a gesture, like the breaking of a dam. Only little by little the full current of his strength began to work. His legs were bent, his back was slightly bowed, and, with all the force in him, he strained until more than a ton's weight of effort drove his feet down into the earth.

The Washburns had smiled; they remained to stare. They heard the creaking of mighty sinews, terribly strained. They heard crackings of bones, as it were. They saw the whole body of this stranger shuddering with his own unleashed power.

And now, with a sudden wrench, he gave the whip snap to his labor. With a ripping sound, with a grinding and a wrenching, the long-embedded stone heaved up from its foundations, while a yell of wonder and dismay came from the Washburns, as though something of their own flesh were being uptorn.

The great boulder staggered, leaned. Its own weight took charge of it, and, toppling over, it rolled with gathering impetus down the brow of the slope, gained speed on the descent, began to leap like a drunken beast, struck a tree, shattered it with a noise like the explosion of a cannon, and then plunged into the creek.

Water leaped up fifty feet in white spray that fell again.

"It's gone!" Mrs. Washburn gasped, coming tottering out from the doorway of the house. "My lands, Pete . . . the table's gone . . . it's gone!"

They stood in awe, the whole family, and stared at the hole from which the great rock had been uprooted. They stared, last of all, at the face of Barney Dwyer, which was covered with a fine perspiration. Threats they would have withstood with their lifeblood. All pleas concerning justice they would have brayed down with mulish and derisive laughter. But here they saw their jest turned into a miraculous and accomplished truth.

They were moved as nothing else in the world could have moved them. The wolfishness was gone from their faces. Like so many children they gaped at Barney Dwyer.

"Jumpin' . . . almighty . . . black-headed . . . thunder," breathed the father of the house.

And after a long moment, Barney said: "You'll send back the steers, Mister Washburn?"

There was a silence.

"Who are you?" asked the oldest son in a hushed voice.

"I'm working on the Parmelee Ranch," said Barney. "Mister Parmelee asked me to come out as his foreman."

The Washburns drew together in a solid group, half of their backs turned to Barney.

But the conference lasted only a moment. He distinguished the guttural tones of the father saying: "And when I see a sign, I reckon I know it."

Then the group quietly dissolved and faced him.

The elder Washburn said: "I know there was some strange cattle come over onto my range. Might be that they're the Parmelee steers. Might be that they're up yonder, now. My boys'll go and take a look at the brands . . . and if they are . . .

I'm gonna have them drove right over onto the Parmelee place."

"Thank you," said Barney. "That's neighborly. Mister Parmelee will appreciate it a lot, I'm sure. Good morning."

He swung into the saddle on the red mare. Silence followed him. Slowly he walked her back across the open ground, very slowly. But presently he heard a crashing of brush, a clacking of hoofs, and, looking back, he saw a herd of young steers break out of the woods behind the Washburn house with three of the Washburn boys on mustangs driving the cattle at full speed straight toward the Parmelee Ranch at the foot of the valley.

VIII

Barney came up with Phil. That worthy cow-puncher was transformed into a staring ghost who looked beyond the new foreman at the miracle of the fifty young steers that were running behind him.

At the verge of the Parmelee lands, the Washburn boys no longer rode behind the cattle, but let them scatter, and Phil it was who skillfully picked them up and drove them bunched before him, as only a good cowman can, straight up toward the Parmelee Ranch house.

Red and Boston Charlie were building fence behind the barn under the immediate eye of Parmelee himself, when Barney came up. He had cantered the red mare well ahead of the returning steers, and, as he approached the barn, first Parmelee and then the two cowpunchers were struck dumb.

Barney reined the mare close by. "Where would you like to have those steers herded?" he asked of Parmelee.

The rancher stared with a hungry eye. "How many are there?" he asked.

"I don't know," said Barney. "I just asked for as many of them as might be on the Washburn land. It didn't occur to me to count them."

"There's fifty of them, all right," said Red. His voice was husky. His eyes seemed to have grown larger, his head smaller, his neck longer, as he stared at the approaching herd and then at the new foreman.

"By God!" broke out Parmelee, "I don't know how you've managed that, but I'll tell you one thing . . . it's the prettiest picture that I ever saw in all of my days. It gives me a sort of hope . . . it gives me a sort of a chance to *dream* that maybe I'll have a fair chance, from now on, to raise cows in these mountains. And if I have that chance, I'm going to raise 'em by the tens of thousands. I'm going to fill the land with beef. I'm going to make a fortune on hides and horns and hoofs and tallow alone."

He saw the whole future burningly before him, and his eyes shone at Barney.

And Barney Dwyer looked calmly back at him and then around the green hills. "There's lots of good grass, around here," said Barney Dwyer.

"Humph!" grunted Parmelee. "How did you get those cows back, anyway?"

"Why, I just asked for them," said Barney. "And then the Washburn boys . . . three of them . . . drove the steers back to the edge of the ranch, and Phil brought them in, as you see. Where do you want them driven, Mister Parmelee?"

"Mister Parmelee," said Bob Parmelee, "wants them left near the ranch house, for a while. He wants them where he can see them for a few days. He wants to fatten his eyes on 'em. You go and put your horse up and go to the house. I'll be in there to talk to you, in a minute."

Barney winced a little. The strength of Parmelee's tone seemed to threaten hard times ahead of him. Was it to be immediate discharge? Slowly he turned the mare and loped her toward the barn, while the three men he had just left eyed one another grimly.

"You started to make a fool of him, Red," said Boston Charlie.

"He seemed to me like a half-wit and a coward," said Red. "And he looked scared just now, Parmelee, when you told him to put up his horse and go to the barn. I dunno what happened at the Washburn place. There's Phil. Call him over."

Phil needed no calling. He came up at a gallop. He dismounted with the face of one who has seen a miracle. "All I know is this," said Phil in a low voice. "I stopped at the edge of the trees, in view of the house. The Washburns was all there. The new boss, he rides up. The five Washburns get up and walk at him. I think that they're gonna knock him on his ear. Then a funny thing happens. You know that big rock in front of the Washburn house? Well, the foreman, he just sashays up to that rock and he tears it out of the ground. . . ."

"Hold on!" said Red. "I've been and seen that rock, and I've handled it. What're you talkin' about . . . tearin' it up?"

"I tell you what I seen with my own eyes, and no liquor aboard me, neither," said Phil. "He done that thing. He tore that rock up, and he threw it down the hill. And it smashed a big tree on the way, and then it landed in the creek, and it knocked the water up as high as the hills, and there it stayed. And I looked to see the Washburn gang turn the boss into a regular colander with their guns, but they didn't do nothin'. And pretty soon three of 'em goes up into the woods behind the house, and they come out ag'in, drivin' the cows before 'em, and they keep right on drivin', until those steers are safe on our land, and I pick 'em up."

Stunned bewilderment greeted this statement.

"What did the foreman say?" asked Red, actually so pale that the freckles stood darkly forth on his face.

"Nothing," said Phil, his voice more subdued than ever. "He acted like it wasn't nothing much that he had done. He come back talkin' more to his red mare, than to me. And I know that what I'm tellin' you was what happened before my eyes . . . unless I was hypnotized, or something."

No one answered him, for an instant, and then Parmelee said: "Well, I had a kind of a hope that something like this might happen. I saw a sort of a dream of it in the back of my head. But I still can't believe that it's true."

They saw Barney go in toward the house. Then a horseman rocked over the top of the nearest hill, and came swinging down toward them, a fine rider, on a fine chestnut horse. He drew rein nearby, and waved his hand.

"It's Leonard Peary!" exclaimed Red. "It's him that used to run with the McGregor gang, till they were broke up by that fellow Barney Dwyer. What's he want up here?"

"Hello, fellows," said Peary. "Hello, Red. Long time no see. I want to know if Barney Dwyer is up here?"

"Dwyer?" shouted Red. "What would he be doing up here? Dwyer?"

"He left Coffeeville to come up here the other day," said Peary. "And I've got news for him."

"Yes," said Parmelee. "He's here."

A sudden shout from Red and from Boston Charley. "Dwyer?" they cried.

Then Red added: "Is that new boss really Barney Dwyer? The red mare . . . my God, I might've known that. I might've known him by his mare. Only, I thought that he'd be bigger. Parmelee, why didn't you tell us? Did you want him to break all our backs?"

"I wanted to wait and see. That's all," answered Parmelee. "I wanted to see how much man he'd show without an introduction. The Washburns seem to think that he's man enough, at any rate."

He left the two to their fence-building, and went to Peary.

"Come over to the house," he said. "I'll take you to Dwyer. But look here, Peary, I thought that you and Dwyer were not friends? I thought you were on the look-out to get him, not long ago?"

"I was," answered Peary instantly. "I was one of the fools who thought that Dwyer is a half-wit. He was too big for me to see, all at once. Then he made me seem like a child, a few times. He saved my life, here and there. Finally I woke up to the fact that he was a great deal better man than I am. And now I've got some bad news for him."

He rode at the side of Parmelee toward the house.

"If you try to get him away from me," said Parmelee, "you'll have to talk big money to him. And you'll have trouble with me, Peary."

"I don't mind who I have trouble with, except with Dwyer," Peary said calmly. "But you can hear the news that I have for him."

He dismounted in front of the ranch house, and there they found Barney Dwyer sitting on the porch and whittling a stick. He jumped up at the sight of Peary, who went toward him with an outstretched hand.

"Barney," he said, "can you let bygones be bygones?"

Barney took the hand at once, very cheerfully. "Why," he said, "I never wanted to be anything but a friend to you, Len. Is there any news?"

"There's the blackest news that you ever heard," said Peary. "Adler set fire to the jail. When the prisoners were taken out, the whole mob of them bolted. Most of them were recaptured, but not Adler and McGregor. They got away. They may be up here already. And they may be picking up a gang to make trouble for you before they arrive. I came on as fast as I could to give you the word. I'm going to stick with you till this trouble is over, if you'll have me."

"Adler and McGregor!" exclaimed Parmelee.

"The devil and the devil's grandfather. Both of 'em loose?"

"Both loose," said Peary grimly. "Maybe you won't want Barney Dwyer so badly now. Because wherever he is, the lightning is pretty sure to strike, before long."

"Did you see Sue?" asked Barney.

"I saw her. She begged me to come here and see the thing through with you."

"Is she safe?" asked Barney, never thinking of himself. "Is anything likely to happen to her?"

"Not if the whole town of Coffeeville can keep trouble away from her," answered Leonard Peary. "The men down there are half crazy because this jail delivery happened. They're watching the girl now like a diamond that might be stolen. No one can bother her, Barney, if all the guns in Coffeeville can keep danger away from her."

"Then I can stay up here," said Barney. "That is, if you still want me, Mister Parmelee."

"Want you?" exclaimed Parmelee. "After you've brought back that whole herd of steers, without one missing? Want you?"

"There's McGregor and the gang he's sure to get together," said Barney. "He'd poison the air of the whole mountains, if he could get rid of me. He'd blow up the whole ranch for you, and never stop to think twice. You understand that?"

"Yes," said Parmelee. "And he'll *have* to blow up the entire ranch to get at you. I'll tell you

193

what, Dwyer . . . we've given you a pretty rough reception, up here. But now we're going to show you what we're made of. My men are a hard lot. But they're men. They wouldn't be here, if they weren't. And by the Lord, Barney Dwyer, we're going to stand by you, shoulder to shoulder, if McGregor, and a thousand devils along with him, try to get at you. Find a single weak-kneed hound on my ranch, and I'll eat his weight in salt."

IX

Events thickened like rain around the Parmelee Ranch that day.

Late in the morning, the father of the Washburn family rode onto the ranch and found Bob Parmelee working at accounts in the house. Old Washburn would not come inside. He sat on his mustang, outside, with a rifle balanced across the horn of his saddle and waited for Parmelee to come out. So Parmelee came, and a gun with him.

Said Washburn: "Parmelee, we ain't been friends."

"I'm never friends with cattle thieves," Parmelee said calmly, watchfully.

"That's a big word and a lot of it," said Washburn. "But I'm here to say that maybe you're gonna change your mind. You got a new man on this ranch of yours, and maybe he's gonna make a whole new outfit. I've come over to talk about him."

"The new foreman?"

"Yes. That's him. He's a whole horse boiled down to the size of a man. Now, Parmelee, me and my family, we've made trouble for you. I ain't denying it. But right from now on, all trouble stops. I ain't a gent that sees many signs, but, when I see 'em, I know what they mean. I seen a sign, this morning bright and early. I'm gonna pay a heed to it, too. Parmelee, what my tribe aims at from now on is friendship. If they's any cattle run off of your place, the last place that you need to look is on my land."

"I'll believe you, Washburn," said the rancher.

"But if you miss cows, they is one thing that you *might* get from us," went on Washburn.

"What's that?"

"News! We might have news for you, and we might give it to you, Parmelee. Times has changed, and we've gone and changed with the times. That's all I wanted to tell you. So long."

He snapped his horse about with a slap of the reins, and loped the cow pony across the hills, and Parmelee, staring after him, saw that the end of his long war seemed to be at hand—if only he could keep Barney Dwyer with him.

The long feud had come to a head and turned in his favor, and Barney Dwyer with a single stroke had made the difference.

At noon, several of the men were far out on the edges of the ranch, their lunches carried with them. Therefore it was not until suppertime that Parmelee made his next effort. He waited until the other men were seated, Peary at the side of Dwyer, and the other ranch hands watching Barney as mice might watch a cat.

Then Parmelee said: "Boys, I guess you all know the name of our new foreman. Last night, you were trying to find out. You tried hard. You tried all the time. But you didn't make the hill. If you'd put on a little more pressure, maybe you would have found out his name, and maybe he would have given you some reasons for remembering it, too."

The men grinned faintly. They looked askance at Barney Dwyer, whose innocent blue eyes were fixed on the face of Parmelee, without malice, almost without understanding. Only Red, pale of face, looked straight down at his plate. He knew that he had seriously offended a famous man, a great warrior. And he felt that a day of reckoning must remain for him.

Parmelee went on: "I think Barney has forgotten what happened last night . . . and part of this morning. I don't think he bears any malice

196

because of a few practical jokes. Do you, Barney?"

Barney started as from a dream, and blushed a little. He was surprised, it seemed, to find himself the center of attention. "No, no," he said. "No malice. A few practical jokes . . . that's all right. No malice to a soul."

Red, hearing this, snapped up his head and looked straight at Barney, and Barney Dwyer smiled a little, and nodded back at him with recognition. Red shunned down a little in his chair with a vast sigh of relief. He would not have gambled on a six months' future for himself, ten minutes before. Now life was given to him; it was like a new birth.

Parmelee went on: "I think you boys know the other news, too. The worst thugs on the entire range, old Adler and McGregor, who were cooped up in jail by Barney Dwyer, are loose again. They're loose and they're sure to come on his trail. Well, boys, that trail has come to a full stop here. Barney Dwyer is here to stay with us, for a while. I think he's broken the back of our cattle war on his first day. And if that's true, he's going to let me make this ranch what it ought to be. It will be a good place for you fellows to work, then. You'll have a chance at more pay in dollars and less in bullets. But before any of us may have a chance at the good things that lie ahead, we've got to make Barney safe here with us. Adler and McGregor are probably near us now. They may be outside the black of those windows this minute, aiming guns at Dwyer."

There was a general start, a loud squeaking and scraping of chairs as heavy bodies moved suddenly in them.

And then Parmelee said: "He's doing his work for us. Our job will have to be to keep McGregor and his gangsters from sinking their bullets in him. Until we've managed to make sure that McGregor and Adler are under the sod or a long distance away from us, we've got to mount guard like soldiers. Are you 'punchers ready to do it?"

They were ready enough. To guard a treasure would mean a fight, and a fight was what most of them were best equipped to enjoy. Besides, to stand with Barney Dwyer was in itself an honor. Not for nothing had the stories of his doings circulated through the mountains in recent days.

It was Red who stood up from the table first. He said: "I made the most trouble for you last night, Barney. Wonder you didn't take and bust me in two. And I'm gonna have the first watch on you. I'm gonna go out and walk the rounds of the house. Keep a scrap of meat and some coffee for me, boys. I'll see that this here supper is quiet enough."

He went to the wall, picked his gun belt from

a peg, buckled it around his hips, settled his hat over his ears, and went straightway out into the darkness.

The others settled down. They felt not a depression but a strength of determination and resource, such as always comes to men who have just banded themselves together. A new friendliness filled them. They looked upon one another with different eyes. Each man appeared to his companions stronger, more valiant, more dependable than ever before.

Leonard Peary glanced swiftly around the table and murmured at the ear of Barney Dwyer: "You don't take long, Barney. One day, and you've made all of these fellows love you. How do you manage it?"

Barney could not have answered. He was utterly confused and bewildered by the strong resolutions that all of these men were taking to insure his safety. And staring about him, he wondered how even the strength of McGregor could break through such a force as this.

He forgot, for the instant, that there is something greater than the prowess of numbers, and that is the weight of brains—and the strength of evil—which has an edge like a poisoned knife.

At this moment there came a loud hail from outside the house. It was the lifted voice of Red. Presently he threw open the door of the house and called out: "Here's a fellow that calls himself

Terry Loftus! Says that he's got a message for you, Dwyer. Have a look at him."

It was a man with a face both fat and firm who stepped through the open door and frowned at the light for an instant. He was not tall. He had a big round body and a small round face. The fat under his skin seemed to have set and fixed in place. If he smiled, it was only a stretching of his lips, and a dimple appeared in either cheek.

He came slowly forward, saying: "Which of you is Dwyer?"

"I am," answered Barney. He stood up and went a step toward Terry Loftus.

"I'm from Coffeeville, and I've got some bad news for you, Dwyer. I've got to tell you . . . I've got to tell you. . . ." His bright, black eyes wandered for an instant. Then he fished out an envelope. "Well, you better read this, first," he said. "Then I'll tell you the rest."

Barney Dwyer opened the letter, which was not addressed, and inside he found a sheet of paper in which a few words were scribbled in the handwriting of Sue Jones. The writing was firm enough in the beginning, but it trailed away to illegibility toward the end. And there was no signature. He read:

Dear Barney,
Blood poisoning has started, they say. And I feel pretty sick. The doctor says

it's dangerous. A man is bringing you this letter because it seems that I ought to say good bye if it takes you too long to . . .

What followed—half a dozen words—was in a scrawl that he could not make out at all. The paper fluttered from his hand to the floor.

Leonard Peary picked it up and stared. Then he groaned.

Barney was saying: "How was she when you left her?"

"Kind of delirious," said Terry Loftus. "She was laying and talking so's you could hear her in the street. Doctor Swain, he says that he's afraid. He's mighty scared. He wants you back there, Dwyer. They asked me to bring you word because I got a fast horse, and I know the way."

"I'm going," said Barney. "I'll go back as fast as the red mare can take me. . . ."

He ran for the door, and disappeared into the night. Terry Loftus followed him, and so did Leonard Peary.

There were no farewells.

But presently, as the men stood about in the dining room, muttering to one another, Red spoke up.

"Any of you ever see that fellow Terry Loftus before?"

A rattling of hoof beats began near the barn and faded down the pass.

"Did *you* ever see him before, Red?" asked Parmelee.

"I'm trying to think," said Red. "Seems like I can remember his face, all right, but I can't spot where I seen it. And I can't spot his name."

Phil broke in: "Did the sight of him make you feel good or bad?"

"Mighty bad," said Red.

"Then he's tucked away for a bad *hombre* somewhere inside of your head," said Phil.

"Take it easy," suggested Parmelee. "Easy does the trick. You can't force your head to work when it don't feel like working."

Red began to stride up and down the room, his head bent, and his brow contorted. "Somebody give me a start," he begged. "I got something so near the tip of my tongue that the roof of my mouth's on fire."

"Sing something, Buck," said Parmelee. "That'll give him a change. Strike up a tune, will you?"

"She was only a bird in a gilded cage. A pitiful sight to see . . . ," began Buck, throwing back his head and letting out a great roar of a voice.

"Wait a minute!" shouted Red. He caught hold of the back of a chair and stared straight before him, entranced by thought. "There was something gilded about it . . . the way I remember him, all right. Now I've got it . . . a big gilded mirror behind a bar . . . and a hard-boiled shack

202

up from the railroad and having some beer . . . and me in a corner and a few more strung along the bar, and then this here fat-faced fellow steps into the picture. He and the railroad operator have a brawl. The fat boy pulls a gun quicker'n a wink and lets the shack have it. The shack meant a fist fight, but the fat boy, he meant murder, and that's what he done. Right through the center of the forehead he drilled that shack and dropped him dead. And the fat boy backed out through the swinging doors. Nobody moved. 'Why don't we go after that killer?' I asked. 'What for?' says the bartender. Wait a minute. I'm remembering the names he used. 'What for,' says the bartender, 'that's Dick Whalen, and he's one of McGregor's men. Want to have McGregor on your back?' "

As Red ended, Parmelee exclaimed: "Boys, if this fellow is packing a wrong name . . . if he worked for McGregor once . . . then he's here to make trouble! He's got Barney Dwyer away from us. I say, we all follow on and try to find out if anything happens on this trail tonight. Will you ride with me?"

There was only one voice, and it sounded like the woof of a bear, but it came from the throat of every man present, and instantly they made a rush for the door of the dining room.

X

Barney was galloping far off, through the night, by this time, with Leonard Peary on his left and the so-called Terry Loftus on his right. When he looked up, the long gallop of the mare made the stars seem to waver in the sky, and out of the night before him, the shapes of hills loomed faintly, and were gone, and trees stood up in strange attitudes, and vanished to the rear. Sometimes Loftus spoke to him. Sometimes Peary. He answered them in words that had no meaning to him. For all that was really in his mind was the girl. He saw that if all of the world was gathered together, all the mountains, the deserts, the rich valleys, all the cities, the farms, the ships, the mighty factories, the mines, the lofty buildings, and all the myriads of people in them, all that was of beauty or of strength—if all of these things were gathered together on the one hand and weighed in divine scales against Sue, for him she would outbalance all the rest. Yes, or even the least attribute or quality of her would be to him more important. That huskiness of her voice that came from laughter, or her smile when she looked at him askance, or a way she had of lifting her head and considering brightly and calmly their future—any of these things would be, to Barney Dwyer, more than the rest of the great universe.

He had suffered much pain, but he never had suffered such pain as this. He had been in terrible danger, and tried to pray, but no prayer had come to his mute lips. But now he prayed. For her sake the words swelled his throat like silent sobbing as he begged the God who rules us to have mercy on Sue Jones. He begged for her life. Then it seemed to him that so much as this could not be granted. He felt that every instant her life was ebbing away. So he only entreated, in that silent agony, that she might endure until he came to the house, and that she might know him, give him some message before the end. That message would be for Barney Dwyer the only important reason for a continued existence in this world.

Those were his thoughts when they came to a place where the valley pinched out to a narrow ravine in which rocks and shrubs crowded the trail on either side.

Suddenly the red mare halted. The violence of her stopping almost threw Barney from the saddle. He urged her forward, as the others drew rein ahead of him to see what was happening. But in spite of her urging, she would not go on. She merely reared and balked, and backed up instead of advancing.

"What's wrong?" Terry Loftus asked smoothly.

"I don't know," said Barney. "She doesn't want to go ahead."

"She smells trouble, then," suggested Peary. "She never acts like a fool, ordinarily. There must be something ahead, Barney. You've told me more than once that she has her reasons."

"What could be ahead?" asked Barney. "She must go on. Go ahead, girl. Get on!"

He slapped her shoulder. The mare merely wheeled in a circle and stood fast, head down, balking resolutely.

"Can't you get your horse on?" Terry Loftus demanded, with heat. "Down there in Coffeeville, there's Sue Jones with the life burnin' out of her and . . ."

Barney groaned. He called out loudly, and suddenly the mare bolted ahead, snorting, shying at the shadows. She swept by Loftus and Peary and was going hard when something hissed in the air above Barney's head, and then he felt the grip of a rope noose that bound his arms against his sides and wrenched him out of the saddle.

He landed with a crash in the midst of a bush. Behind him, he heard the yell of Peary and the barking of a gun. But as he stood up, he saw that Peary's horse, too, had an empty saddle.

Men rushed in on either side. They spun the lariat around him, until he was fast imprisoned. And he heard the voice of Doc Adler saying:

"Good work, Terry Loftus. Brains. That's what you got. Brains!"

Then McGregor came and stood by him. He knew it was McGregor by the familiar outline of the shoulders, and the head canted a trifle to the side. And he felt that he would know it for McGregor even by the breathing of the man. McGregor said nothing, simply devouring his prisoner in silent glance.

Then, as he turned away, other men threw Barney like a sack of bran over the saddle on the back of the mare, and they were led off.

Barney had uttered no complaint. When he considered the profound depth of the hatred of McGregor, such a thing as speech between them became a folly. It was Peary who cried out in lamentation, and who cursed Terry Loftus.

Loftus rode up beside the horse that was carrying Peary, and Barney saw the hand of Loftus fly up, heard the whacking and cutting noise of a lash as it landed.

"You damn' traitor," said Loftus. "What you talkin' to me about, anyway? I'm true to my kind, and you're a dirty turncoat!"

They left the trail well behind them, turned through a wilderness of rocks and trees, and so came close to the sound of running water.

They entered a little cove, a pleasant green place with a smooth floor and a hedging of bushes and trees about it, and the rushing of water at its side, with a little lean-to built near the edge of the creek. The noise of the water was like the noise of the wind by the sea.

Into the lean-to they took Barney and Peary and flung them down on the floor. A lantern was found and lit. The illumination showed a tumble-down wreck of a place, and yet there was a lantern and oil in the shed. Barney was able to wonder at that.

His mind began to detach from his body. He felt as he had when he was a child, enduring cold on an endless ride by night, or listening to the talk of grown men while sleep benumbed his brain. He could forget fear, almost, and watch the faces of the brutal men around him, and see their grinning eyes.

McGregor had Adler and five other men with him. They were like wolves, and as wolves do, so they hunted in packs.

McGregor said: "You fellows scatter. I want to be alone here with Adler and these two old friends of mine. Get out of here and put your-selves where you can be on the watch."

"What we gonna watch for?" asked Terry Loftus.

"Watch for trouble," snapped McGregor. "Wherever this half-wit of a Dwyer goes, he makes friends. You never can tell what may happen."

The men left the place to Adler, McGregor, and those two helpless prisoners.

McGregor took the lantern and shone its light into the face of Barney.

"Turn pale, damn you," he said.

Barney looked straight at the light, not at the man who held it. He studied the crookedness of the wick, and the crooked flame that rose from it. He saw the rusted metal of the hail of the lantern, and the jagged crack down one side of the chimney. He was not thinking. He was simply seeing.

"Look at him," said McGregor.

Old Doc Adler came, like a humpbacked buzzard, and sat on his heels and stared into Barney's face.

"His eyes, they ain't changed none," said Adler.

"I'll change 'em before I'm through," said McGregor.

"You take pale blue eyes like them," said Adler, "and sometimes they don't change none. Not even when they die. They're like steel in the color of them, and they're strong as steel, too. Maybe they won't change none."

"Damn you!" breathed McGregor, and kicked Barney in the face.

The toe of the boot landed fairly on the jaw of Barney. It struck red sparks from his brain. That was all. He was not surprised or appalled. This was nothing, compared with his expectations.

They would tear him to pieces, the pair of them. They would shred him small.

It was Peary who cried out, when he saw that brutal indignity offered to his friend. "Stop it!" shouted Peary. "You rotten pair of coyotes!"

McGregor poised a quirt, but delayed the blow. "I don't know," he said. "We don't want to waste much time on this one."

Adler went to Peary, and sat on his heels again until his face was level with that of Peary, who was propped against the wall.

"Well," said Adler, "suit yourself. This here is a different sort of a gent. This here is the sort of a pair of eyes that would open up, when he started to screaming. That's what they'd do. They'd open up." He began to chuckle, nodding that old head of his until the hair flashed to silver in the lantern light.

"Would he scream?" McGregor asked carelessly.

"Yeah. He'd break down. He ain't got the nerve that lasted. This here Dwyer, he's got the nerve of a bulldog. The more you beat him, the harder he'd hang on. But Peary, he's just a flash. He's a wildcat. He's good for one spring, and then he's through."

"Is he?" asked McGregor, carelessly still. "Well, I don't want to waste time on him. He's not the one who's been on my mind. He's a dirty traitor. That's all. And he's going to get what comes to traitors. He's not on my mind. Dwyer is the one we've been thinking about. Eh, Doc?"

"Yeah. We been thinking a little about Barney Dwyer," agreed Doc Adler. He stood up and turned toward Barney, and licked his gray, dry lips.

"Peary!" called out McGregor.

"Well?" Leonard Peary said calmly enough.

"You know what I do to traitors, Peary?"

"You shoot 'em," said Peary.

"And I'm going to shoot you!"

Peary nodded.

"Unwind that rope from his legs. Let him stand up," said McGregor.

"Why?" asked Adler. "Shoot him the way he is."

"I want to see him drop, when I shoot," said McGregor.

"That's the trouble with you Scotch gents," said Adler. "You got a lot of sentimentality in you, that's what you got. You're like poets, is what you're like. You wanna make things into pretty pictures. This here Peary dead, is what you want. Ain't that enough? You got to see him drop, too? Well, well, well, well. When I was around in the world, I didn't go and waste my time like that, McGregor. But have it your own way." He was unwrapping the legs of Peary as he spoke. "Stand up," he said.

Peary had been half numbed, so that he could

not move quickly. Adler turned his foot and drove the long rowels of his spur into the side of the boy.

"Up, old horse," Adler said, and laughed.

Peary rose to his feet. Barney, sickened, closed his eyes.

"Look," said the voice of McGregor. "Look, Doc. That's what he can't stand."

"Yeah," said Adler. "His nerves they run right out into the body of this here Peary, maybe. Well, well, well." He chuckled again.

"Peary," said McGregor, "you're going to die . . . now!"

"I'm better dead than one of your gang," said Peary.

"He's turning good," McGregor said. "Listen to him, Adler. He's one of the curs that get religion before they're hanged. They repent and they confess when they've got a rope around their necks."

"Yeah, and I've seen and heard 'em do it, and it's a funny thing, all right," commented Adler. He shook his head in the wonder of it.

"I'd give you some special attention," said McGregor, "instead of bumping you off like this. I'd set you to screaming until the boys who are waiting out there would take a warning and a lesson by what they heard. There'll be no more traitors in my gang, for a while."

Peary was stone-white. Barney could see

that, clearly, and he wondered at the change in his friend. And yet like a stone, Len Peary was steady.

"Your gang is about finished, Mack," said Peary.

"Finished, eh? What makes you think that?"

"You used to be a great man, Mack," said Peary. "But you're a great man no longer. There was a time when men used to think that you couldn't be beaten. You were a superman. That's what I felt about you. I knew you were a robber, but I thought, as a kid, that you were not exactly bad. You were a Robin Hood, in my eyes. Not bad, but simply strong. That's why I joined you. I was a fool. I thought I was doing a great thing, when I was able to join you. I thought it was a high adventure, and all that. I was proud. So were most of the rest who worked for you. But the old crowd is gone. Look what you've picked up now . . . throat-cutters, and second-story thugs. Bums and loafers and deadbeats and mangy dogs, compared with the men you used to have. Put me in a room with all five of those yellow hounds, and I'll clean them out. You know I will. But you're gone, McGregor. You're not a Robin Hood any more. You're just a plain robber and murderer. Barney Dwyer opened the windows and let in the light on you, and the whole world knows about you now. The ranch boys don't read about you and talk about you. They have a new hero. They have a real hero. And that's Barney Dwyer."

"Are you through?" McGregor asked in a terrible voice.

"I could make a pretty long speech," said Peary. "But I've said enough to let you know why I'd rather die right here and now than be free and live to work with you again."

"Die, and be damned, then," said McGregor, gasping out the words through his teeth. He jerked out a gun and fired—one smooth, blindingly fast movement.

It was to Barney as though he had seen lightning strike. Poor Leonard Peary dropped on his face and lay still.

XI

There was an odd thing, now, for any man to see, which was that the great McGregor, instead of giving even a second glance to his victim, turned on his heel and looked sharply at Barney Dwyer.

But Barney was contemplating infinitely distant space. He was no longer in this world. There would be some pain, but he was used to pain of body and mind. It might be a long and dreadful frontier, but he would pass it, and reach peace.

Leonard Peary must be already there, in that peace. A man who could face death in that manner could not be unrewarded by whatever powers may be.

McGregor snarled: "He doesn't feel it, Adler."

"He'll feel something else, though," said Adler. "I've got some ideas in my head that he'll feel, and don't you doubt it." He chuckled, and warmed his skinny claws by chafing them together.

The red mare whinnied, her voice inside the room. She was standing at the doorway, looking with puzzled eyes at her master.

"Look there, now," said Adler, pleased by the sight of that beautiful head. "There's a horse, now, that would just about die for her master, if she knowed what was goin' on. But she don't know. She don't know no more than a baby in a cradle. So she stands there, and sings out to him, and there ain't a word that he can speak, and there ain't a sign that he can make to her. And that's a thing that I could set down and watch for a considerable time." He kept on chuckling, as he spoke.

It seemed to Barney that these two men were pictures out of old books, representing the ultimate evil. Old painters and engravers were never tired of showing the devils of hell as goat-like, evil old men, and crime-hardened, smooth-faced tormentors, master fiends with the face of McGregor. The comparison was of interest to Barney.

"Try Peary," said McGregor. "See if he's really dead."

Adler stalked to the fallen body, took Peary by the hair, and lifted the head. The mouth gaped open loosely, the eyes were open, too, mere slits as dull as the dead eyes of a fish. Adler dropped the head. It bounced a trifle on the floor.

"He's dead," said Adler.

"Listen to his heart," McGregor said.

"Did you see the hole in the middle of his forehead?" asked Adler.

"Oh, is that it?" McGregor said.

"When I was your age," Adler said, frowning, "I knowed where I was shootin'. I didn't have to go and look. I *knowed* where the bullet went. It was my business to know."

"You and your ages be damned," said McGregor. "Here's our main job, Doc. We've brushed the small things out of the way, and now we can give a little attention to Mister Barney Dwyer, the hero!"

"We can give him some attention," Adler agreed, nodding.

"I've got some ideas borrowed from Indians," said McGregor.

"Don't go and be backward, like that," urged Adler. "This here world keeps on progressin'. Go clean back to the red skins? No, sir. I got better ideas than the Indians ever had in all their lives, the devils. I could show you some things that'd warm up your heart for you, Mack."

"I'll bet you could, Doc," McGregor said, highly pleased. "And I'm as willing to learn as a boy at school from an old schoolteacher. Go right ahead and use that brain of yours."

"It ain't a thing to hurry with," said Doc Adler.

There was a broken-down chair, in the room. He pulled this out to the center of the floor and sat down in it, facing Barney, studying him like a problem in geometry.

"This here," said Doc Adler, "is the sort of a thing that a gent had oughta set and study over, and work over, and think out, and smoke, and think, and smoke, and get the right ideas." He filled a pipe as he spoke, tamping the tobacco in hard. Then he scratched a match and puffed seriously, shielding his eyes a little from the smoke by a frown and a squint.

When the pipe was well kindled, he went on, driving the smoke out of one corner of his vast mouth, and the words out of the other corner: "This here life of Dwyer is only one life. It's like the last match for the lightin' of a fire. Once that life is burned out, there ain't no way that you can start it again. Once he's dead, there ain't gonna be no way we can bring him to life ag'in and kill him ag'in in a longer and a better method. When he's dead, he's dead. So we gotta kill him the best way. The way that's gonna leave the longest and the best taste in your mouth, afterward."

"Go on, Doc," said McGregor in approval. "I agree with everything."

"You've done us a lot of harm, Barney," said Doc Adler, sadly shaking his head.

"Yes," said the gentle voice of Barney. "I believe that I *have* done you a lot of harm."

"He sounds sorry for it," Adler said, interested.

"Damn him," said McGregor. "You'll have to hurry with your ideas a little, Doc. When I think what he's done, I want to get my hands on him."

"And hands ain't a bad idea, neither," said Doc Adler. "Maybe handwork is the best way to finish him, but I ain't so sure. I wanna think things out. The fact is, you done us a lot of harm, Barney. Here's Mack, now, that was the kingpin in these here mountains. He was pointed to by the crooks as the king of them all. He was pointed at by the honest men as a gent that had covered up his trail so well that he'd never been even once in jail. And now look at him. Look at him!"

"Shut up. That's enough!" snapped McGregor.

"Well," said Doc Adler, "maybe it *is* enough, because I reckon that Peary put it about right. You've started downhill, Mack, and, from now on, you're gonna go to hell fast. Year or two, it wouldn't surprise me if you was washin' dishes for a Chink cook and eatin' the scraps off of plates for your food."

McGregor made a nervous gesture, and said

nothing. Adler grinned at him, but then went on: "As for me, there was old Doc Adler that had retired. And nobody had nothin' on *him,* neither. They just knowed that he'd been around the world a mite . . . quite a mite! But they didn't have nothin' on old Doc Adler. Not until he throwed in with McGregor to put down Barney Dwyer. And then everything went wrong, and poor old Doc Adler, he's gotta put a bullet through his head, rather than be caught by the police. Because they'd jail him for the rest of his days, because of the mess he's got into in his old days. And that's all because of you, Barney Dwyer."

"I'm afraid it is," said Barney, sighing a little.

McGregor burst out: "Do something, Doc, before I throttle him . . . the damned half-wit!"

"Well," Adler said, "*he's* the one that could do a good, quick job of throttlin', when you come to that. He's got the hands for it. He could squash out the life with one grip of them terrible hands of his. Which makes me think . . . suppose that we was to start with his right hand, so long as we don't think of nothin' better."

"How do you mean?" asked McGregor.

"Kill his right hand for him, while the rest of him is still alive."

"I don't follow that."

"Suppose that we wrap his right hand in a bit of cloth and soak that there cloth in some kerosene. And then touch a match to it. That would burn the flesh off his bones, and we could set and study. And by the light of that there burnin' hand, Mack, we might see our way clear through to something worthwhile."

McGregor strained his head suddenly back and stared up at the ceiling. "Ah, Doc," he said. "I was wondering if it were worthwhile to wait, like this. But now I see that it *is* right. You've found one perfect thing to do. We'll think of other things, for other parts of him. Unfasten that right hand . . . but treat it like dynamite."

That, in fact, was what they did. They held a gun at the head of Barney while they freed his right forearm from the ropes. McGregor then ripped the shirt from the back of the prostrate body of Peary, and that cloth was tightly wrapped around the hand of Dwyer and soaked with kerosene from the lantern.

Doc Adler sat on his heels and looked into the eyes of Dwyer.

"They ain't changed. His eyes ain't changed, Mack," he announced regretfully. "Seems like he's quite a man, Mack. How come, Barney? What holds you together? If you ain't sad about yourself, what about that pretty gal, that loves you so much?"

"I never was worthy of her," said Barney.

"Scratch a match, Mack," Adler said.

It was done. McGregor, smiling with a terrible and hungry joy, held the match to wait for final

220

instructions from Adler, who seemed such a master hand at this business.

"We touch this here match to the rag," said Adler, "and that's the end of your right hand, Barney. A dog-gone' famous right hand it is, too. There ain't a man in the mountains that would dare to stand up to that hand, nor any two men, neither. And now it's gonna go up in smoke, and who'll make up the difference to you, Barney?"

"There is God," Barney said slowly.

"By the jumping thunder, he's got religion!" exclaimed Adler. "And that spoils everything! What makes you think there's a God?"

"I was never sure before," Barney said truthfully.

"And what makes you sure now?" demanded McGregor, scowling blackly.

"I don't know," answered Barney. "It's seeing people like you two, I suppose. There would have to be a God to make up the difference."

"Damn him," McGregor hissed as the match went out against the tender tips of his fingers. "I knew that he'd sink a knife in us, some way."

"It's religion that does it, Mack," commented Adler. "You find it where you don't expect it, and you can't never beat it, I've noticed. It's a funny thing that you can't never beat it."

Rapid footfalls swept toward them.

"Mack!" called a voice.

McGregor hurried to the door of the shed.

Barney, looking vaguely before him, saw something move on the floor. It was the hand of Peary. It contracted slowly, and opened again!

And a golden bolt of hope darted through the noble soul of Barney Dwyer, not a hope for his own safety, but that the life of Peary might endure, after all.

"There's half a dozen men up on the trail," said a voice in the outer darkness.

"Half a dozen. What about 'em? Let 'em go," said McGregor.

"Maybe they ain't inclined to go," said the other. "They're flashin' lights on the trail, and studyin' sign. Might be that they're lookin' for us, eh?"

"If they're looking for us . . . we'll blow them to hell. I won't have this job spoiled in the middle." He added: "Go back up to the trail, and watch with the rest of 'em. I'm following on."

The footsteps retreated.

McGregor turned back into the room. "Tie that hand against his body again, Doc," he commanded. "We'll go up there and see what's what."

"Suppose we come back and find this gent gone?" complained Adler, busily obeying instructions, nonetheless.

"He might roll as far as the door . . . that's all," said McGregor. "Don't be a fool."

"I don't like it," answered Doc Adler. "There's

a pricklin' up my spine that makes me not like it. But . . . you're the boss, Mack."

So the right forearm of Barney was once again gathered in the invincible strength of the ropes against his body, and McGregor left the place. At the door, he paused to strike at the head of the red mare. Then he ran on.

"Hey, Len!" Barney called cautiously.

He received no answer. He rolled himself across the floor to his friend, and called at his ear: "Peary!"

A faint groan answered him.

"Peary, can you wake up . . . can you cut the ropes on me?" pleaded Barney.

A faint sigh answered him, and he knew that there was no hope of rousing the unconscious body of Peary to give him a single stroke of help.

XII

They would be back before long, he could be sure.

He looked around for help. So much as a sharp-edged nail might be enough, projecting from the wall, for him to chafe through a few strands of the rope until he could snap it with a great effort of his arms.

But there was not a sign of anything that faintly resembled a tool. Nothing was near him on which he could look with pleasure, except the bright eyes of the red mare, in the doorway.

He rolled toward her, never thinking of what he could manage when he reached her, and, as he floundered forward, she actually stepped through the doorway, and stood there, whinnying a little, her knees bent with terror, at finding herself inside this enclosure with the smell of blood in the air, but her affectionate soul drawn by the sight of her master, the god-like man, wallowing toward her like some strange earth-bound animal.

Barney heaved himself to a half-erect sitting position. It was the limit of his ability to move. If once he could reach that saddle, he could guide her by word of mouth wherever he pleased. But he might as well have hoped to leap on the back of an eagle.

She stamped on the floor. A cloud of dust rose into his face, and the stirrups flopped just above his head. That was what gave him the idea. He caught the leather edge of the stirrup in his teeth, and hissed softly at her.

The red mare whirled and bounded out of that place of doom like a thunderbolt, almost wrenching the teeth from Barney's head, and leaving him behind.

When he recovered from the shock, he worked his way, snake-like, through the doorway into the open. His voice called her back, still trembling and uneasy. And again she snuffed at him, and again the whinny came from her throat as softly as a human voice.

He gained the strategic position again. Then, lifting his body as well as he could, he gained a firmer grip of the edge of the stirrup. He made a faint sound in the hollow of his throat, and the mare moved. The strain of the starting almost disengaged his hold, but the strength that was in all parts of his body was not lacking in the mighty grasp of his jaw. Like the bulldog to which old Doc Adler had compared him, he kept his hold, and the mare dragged him over the grass.

She stopped. He heard the rattle of her bridle as she shook her head. Again he groaned forth a stifled order, and again she went on. She stepped forth at a brisk walk, and his body slid easily over the grass.

Every step from that lean-to was a step toward salvation. And with a vast incredulity he found himself drawn up to the verge of the brush, and then through a gap in it. He had taught her to go by gee and haw. Those words he used now, bringing them out of his throat without much difficulty in spite of the fact that his teeth were locked. So he guided her well to the left. For straight above them would be those waiting watchers of the gang of McGregor, and he would have to attempt to cut around to the side of them.

His hope was to find the other men—the group of six who were searching the trail.

So he guided her, and she dragged him steadily up until they came to the rocks. Half a dozen times, a projecting stone caught at his shoulder and broke the grip of his teeth. A tooth snapped off short. Blood filled his mouth. But he was hardly sensible of it, or of the pain.

Faith, which had been born in him full-grown in the shed, in the presence of death, had grown to a giant in his soul, now that he had the hope of life. Again and again he resumed his grip on the stirrup leather, and again and again the mare, having lost him, came back to his voice. She began to learn her work. She began to avoid obstacles against which she might drag that precious burden that trailed behind.

A sound of steps came near him. He stopped the mare with a whisper and lay still. Horses were moving by him. He saw nothing, but he heard the grinding of the iron shoes against the rocks.

Then two voices.

"They won't find nothin'."

"If they do, we'll be gone."

"McGregor's killed Peary."

"Yeah. But Peary's the lucky one, I reckon."

And they laughed, both of them.

But the night covered the sound of the horses, rapidly. Once more Barney could resume that strange progress. It brought him up, at last, onto the trail. The clothes on his back and sides had been ripped to tatters. His flesh was raw, in many a place. But that hardly mattered, when he saw far away the gleam of a light. Whoever searched that trail was not a friend of McGregor. That was certain, and that was all he wished to know.

So he raised his voice to a shout, to a thundering outcry that beat far away in echo on echo. "Help! Help! This way! Help!"

The light staggered and disappeared. There was a rush of hoof beats. He shouted again, and suddenly around him was a swirl of horsemen.

"Who's there?" called the voice of Parmelee.

"Barney Dwyer," he answered.

They gave one wild yell of satisfaction and rage, commingled. In an instant he was free, he was lifted. Furious inquiries poured on him.

But Barney was already in the saddle on the red mare.

"Parmelee," he said, "Loftus was a liar. McGregor sent him. I suppose that Sue's letter was forged. But down there in a shack is Peary . . . and perhaps some of the rest of them." And he added: "Will you follow me?"

"To hell and back!" shouted the voice of Red.

And Barney drove the mare frantically back over the ground he had just covered so painfully, inch by inch.

They swept through the brush and rocks, and they came beating out on the level of the grass.

Were the men of McGregor waiting for the attack, hidden like so many Indians? No, but far away the hoofs of their horses were pounding.

From the shed burned the light of the lantern, still. That was the first goal. Out of the saddle, and into the doorway, in time to see a frightful picture of poor Len Peary lifting himself from the floor, with glazed eyes like the eyes of the dead, and a horrible red wound that slanted from the center of his forehead up into his hair. It must have been a glance wound. There was no other explanation for the life in that half-conscious body.

But the life was there. That was the main thing. The life was in him, and yonder were the beating hoofs of the horses that carried the men of McGregor away. They must not escape. It was not mere anger that filled Barney. It was a coldness of resolution, like the coldness of steel.

"Leave one man, Parmelee," he begged, "and the rest come on with me. I've got to find McGregor before this trail ends."

XIII

There was not a man of them all who did not ride as well as his horse would carry him, on that night. But the difference was that their horses galloped, and the red mare flew. And a ragged half-moon rose in the east, and looked down

228

the narrow ravine through which the men of McGregor were fleeing.

Barney was hardly aware that his friends were dropping behind him. He only knew that he was gaining rapidly on the scurrying forms that ran ahead.

Two of them rode side-by-side, last of all. Would they fight? Not they. Well had Peary announced the quality of those who followed the diminished fortunes of McGregor now. He had snatched a revolver that was thrust into his hands by one of the men from the Parmelee Ranch—Red, was it not?—and now he fired high in the air.

The two rascals nearest at hand screeched as though the bullet had driven through both their bodies. They drew up and turned, and lifted their hands high above their heads, and yelled for mercy.

But Barney drove headlong past them.

They were nothing. They were the ciphers without meaning, once McGregor were removed.

And McGregor was there.

Off to the sides scurried three more, before the charge of the red mare, and now remained only two. He could swear that they were the great McGregor, and terrible old Doc Adler.

But even Adler hardly mattered. He was old, and time would soon end him, no doubt. But McGregor was young. He must be slain as a wolf is slain when there are sheep in the pasture lands.

The small ravine gave into a larger one with great broken walls that fenced, high above them, a narrow street through the sky, but still the valley held toward the east, and therefore the moon shone down into it.

And still the red mare gained, running with a deathless courage, faster and faster, as though she understood very well the meaning of this race. She did not need watching. She would pick her footing among the loose rocks that were scattered over the floor of the valley. No wild mountain goat could be surer of foot than was she.

But not so one of the nearing horses of the pair ahead. It staggered, toppled, and leaped again to its feet. On the ground, prostrate, remained the long body of Adler, with the moon glinting on his hair. He was raising himself, crawling slowly to his feet, as though stunned, when Barney drove past. Nothing could have been easier than to drive a bullet through that murderous old man, but the finger of Barney Dwyer would not close over the trigger.

A strange passion came over him. There was a roar of water from the deep of the ravine. It entered his brain like the shouting of voices. The moon seemed to him to be hung divinely in the sky to give him light for his purpose. There was no doubt in him. It seemed to him now that from the first he had been merely a tool to be used in breaking McGregor. And now he would finish the work. He would have charged on if a hundred men were there to stand beside the bandit.

The red mare knew that the end was near. She redoubled her efforts as the fugitive's horse began to lose strength. Twice McGregor turned his head. Then he pulled up and turned his horse, and the long barrel of his rifle flashed in the moonlight as he unsheathed it.

He might as well have made a gesture with a straw, as far as Barney was concerned. For he drove straight in, balancing his revolver for the distant shot.

The rifle bullet sang past his head, with the clap of the report behind it.

Still he closed on McGregor, with the revolver poised and ready in his hand.

A second time the rifle spoke, and again the fickle moonlight made McGregor miss.

But before the third chance for McGregor, Barney Dwyer fired. It seemed as though horse and man had been slain outright, they dropped in such a heap. But it was only the mustang that had suffered with a bullet through the head.

As Barney came up, he saw McGregor struggle free, stagger, and then turn to fight his last. If the revolver ever came into the magic hand of McGregor, there could only be one termination to the battle, and Barney, as he swung out of the saddle, gripped the outlaw with both hands.

As a great electric current paralyzed a strong man, so McGregor was paralyzed. He struggled vainly. He flung his head from side to side. But Barney held him like a child.

At last McGregor knew, and stood still. Only his face worked, as words came up to his lips, and were denied utterance. What could he say?

"Barney," he gasped at last, "for Christ's sake give me a last chance. I would have murdered you. But you were ready to die. And I'm no more ready than a black dog. Barney, don't kill me with those hands of yours."

"McGregor," said Barney, "don't whine. You've lived and fought and killed. You've been what you thought a man should be. You ought to die like a man. And I've got to kill you."

"Don't kill me, Dwyer!" shouted McGregor. "Barney, I can make you rich. I've got enough money. . . ."

Unable to meet the terror in that face, Barney had looked away, down the smooth descent of rock on which they stood to the verge of the creek's channel, where the spray leaped like the pale lashes of a thousand whips.

Now, with a groan of disgust, he suddenly stepped back and thrust McGregor from him, exclaiming: "You're not fit to live, McGregor, but in my mind, you're not fit to die, either. I can't kill a coward!"

So he had exclaimed, casting McGregor from

him, and hearing the outlaw groan with relief.

Then chance took its turn in the game. That slope of rock to the verge of the inner ravine was wet and slippery with the spray that had been thrown up by the stream, and the boots of McGregor slipped on the surface as though it were oiled. He put down a hand to stop the sliding. It was in vain. Suddenly he realized that he was barely set free from death in one way, to be delivered to it in another.

He cast himself face down, spreading out his arms with such a screech as Barney Dwyer would never forget. But the descent was too swift, and the surface of the rock too slippery. A jutting rock stopped the slide of McGregor for an instant and brought him to his feet. But he reeled backward. For an instant he beat at the air with his hands and his terrible face was silvered by the moon for Barney to see. Then he was gone.

Barney, shaking in all his body, worked his way down to the edge of the rock.

That was where the men from the Parmelee Ranch found him—stretched prone and looking down into the furious uproar, the wild beating of the water and the leaping of the foam.

They had gathered in the gang of McGregor as fishermen gather up little fish from the sea. Only old Doc Adler had slipped through their fingers.

But Barney Dwyer felt no exultation. He was silent all the way into the town of Coffeeville, where the Parmelee cowpunchers brought their prisoners.

The moon turned into a pale tuft of cloud, before they reached the town. The dawn began. In the rose of it they entered Coffeeville, but not too early to be seen and observed.

So the news ran riot through the little place. McGregor was dead. He had escaped only to die at once, more horribly than the death that the law would have given him. McGregor was dead. Doc Adler, alone, would hardly be more than a twigless snake, to be sure. And as for the harm done by McGregor's last efforts, there was only Leonard Peary to account for, and he was now lying in the hospital in Coffeeville recovering as fast as rest and medicine could make him.

He would be marked for life, to be sure. But, as he said to Barney Dwyer: "I had it coming to me. If I hadn't been marked, it would have been wrong. I deserved a lot worse than I got."

Barney studied that thought, but finally he shook his head. "I don't know," he said. "There's justice, somewhere, and there's a judge. I felt it out there in the lean-to. I felt that I was being judged, and McGregor and Adler were being judged. And no matter what we do or how far or how fast we run, we never can get away from *that* sort of a judgment, Len."

He stood up.

"My father's in the next room. He wants to see you," said Peary.

Barney considered.

"I used to think," he said at last, "that I wanted nothing so much as to get back there to the ranch, and be among those cowpunchers again. But I've been changing my mind, Len. I've changed my mind about a lot of things. I don't blame people for what they used to do to me. But I don't want to see them again. You tell your father that, and I think that he'll understand."

He went down the stairs and to the back of the hotel. Through the back door he escaped into the lane, and so, by devious paths, afraid that the crowd might see him, he returned to the house of Dr. Swain.

Sue Jones was sitting up straight in her easy chair in the garden. And Robert Parmelee was sitting beside her, talking hard and fast, making eager gestures, leaning toward her.

A certain coldness came over the mind of Barney. For Parmelee talked like a man making love, and the girl listened as though she were moved to her heart, for her eyes were closed and there was a tender smile on her lips.

Slowly Barney approached.

Big Parmelee stood up and greeted him. "I've got the whole future blocked out, Barney," he said. "You're going up there and take a part of my land. That's to be your beginning. Rustling is

235

going to die . . . the rustlers are going to clear out, when they know that you're around. You'll be my foreman on a fat salary, and you'll boss your own herds, and Sue will boss you. Tell me, Barney, if that makes a happy future?"

Barney Dwyer smiled, but looked quickly at the girl. She did not even open her eyes, but held out a hand toward him.

"What do you say to it, Sue?" he asked her.

"Nothing," said the girl. "I don't care what happens, or what we do. We could sit and drift, I think, and everything would be sure to come out right in the end. These mountains were made for you, and you were made for the mountains. Any other air is too thick for a mountain man."

Sun and Sand

Although Faust continued to write for Street & Smith's *Western Story Magazine* through 1935, by 1933 his output was being published in a variety of publications, including *Argosy*, *McCall's Magazine*, and *Collier's*. "Sun and Sand" was his penultimate story in *Western Story Magazine*, appearing in the issue dated February 16, 1935, under his Hugh Owen byline. The protagonist, Jigger, is similar to several of Faust's youthful heroes—Speedy and Reata—in that he is able to outwit and outmaneuver even the deadliest of men without the use of a gun.

I

At the pawnbroker's window, Jigger dismounted. He had only a few dollars in his pocket, but he had an almost childish weakness for bright things, and he could take pleasure with his eyes even when he could not buy his fancy. But on account of the peculiar slant of the sun, the only thing he could see clearly, at first, was his own image. The darkness of his skin startled him. It was no wonder that some people took him for a Gypsy or an Indian. He was dressed like a Gypsy vagrant, too, with a great patch on one shoulder of his shirt and one sleeve terminating in tatters at the elbow.

However, he was not one to pride himself on appearance. He stretched himself; his dark eyes closed in the completeness of his yawn. Then he pressed his face closer to the window to make out what was offered for sale.

There were trays of rings, stick pins, jeweled cuff links. There were four pairs of pearl-handled revolvers, some hatbands of Mexican wheelwork done in metal, a little heap of curiously worked conchos, a number of watches, silver or gold, knives, some fine lace, yellow with age, a silver tea set—who had ever drunk tea in the mid-afternoon in this part of the world?—an odd bit of Mexican feather work, spurs of plain steel, silver, or gold, and a host of odds and ends of all sorts.

The eye of Jigger, for all his apparently lazy deliberation, moved a little more swiftly than the snapping end of a whiplash. After a glance, he had seen this host of entangled curiosities so well that he would have been able to list and describe most of them. He had settled his glance on one oddity that amused him—a key ring that was a silver snake that turned on itself in a double coil and gripped its tail in its mouth, while it stared at the world and at Jigger with glittering little eyes of green.

Jigger went to the door, and the great golden stallion from which he had dismounted started to follow. So he lifted a finger and stopped the horse with that small sign, then he entered.

The pawnbroker was a foreigner—he might have been anything from a German to an Armenian—and he had a divided beard that descended in two points, gray and jagged as rock. He had a yellow, wrinkled forehead, and his thick glasses made two glimmering obscurities of his eyes. When Jigger asked to see the silver snake key ring, the bearded man took up the tray that contained it.

"How much?" asked Jigger.

"Ten dollars," said the pawnbroker.

"Ten which?" asked Jigger.

"With emeralds for eyes, too. But I make it seven fifty for such a young man."

Jigger did not know jewels, but he knew men.

"I'll give you two and a half," he said.

"I sell things," answered the pawnbroker. "I can't afford to give them away."

"Good bye, brother," Jigger said, but he had seen a shimmer of doubt in the eyes of the other and he was not surprised to be called back from the door.

"Well," said the pawnbroker, "I've only had it in my window for two or three hours. It's good luck to make a quick sale . . . so here you are."

And as Jigger laid the money on the counter, he commenced to twist off the keys.

"Hold on," said Jigger. "Let the tassels stay on it, too. They make it look better."

"You want to mix them up with your own keys?" asked the pawnbroker.

"I haven't any keys of my own," said Jigger, laughing, and went from the pawnshop at once.

As he walked down the street, the stallion followed him, trailing a little distance to the rear, and people turned to look at the odd sight, for the horse looked fit for a king, and Jigger was in rags. There were plenty of men in the streets of Tucker Flat, because, since the bank robbery of three months ago, the big mines in the Chimney Mountains north of the town had been shutting down one by one. They never had paid very much more than the cost of production, and the quarter million stolen from the Levison Bank had consisted chiefly of their deposits. Against that blow the three mines had struggled but failed to recover. And the result was that a flood of laborers was set adrift. Some of them had gone off through the mountains in a vain quest for new jobs; others loitered about Tucker Flat in the hope that something would happen to reopen the mines. That was why the sheriff had his hands full. Tucker Flat always was as hard as nails, but now it was harder still.

The streets were full, but the saloons were empty, as Jigger soon observed when he went into one for a glass of beer. He sat at the darkest corner table, nursing the drink and his gloomy thoughts. Doc Landy had appointed this town and that evening as the moment for their meeting, and only the devil that lived in the brain of the pseudo peddler could tell what new and dangerous task Landy would name for Jigger.

He had been an hour in the shadows, staring at his thoughts, before the double swing doors of the saloon were pushed open by a man who looked over the interior with a quick eye, then muttered: "Let's try the red-eye in here, old son."

With a companion, he sauntered toward the bar, and Jigger was at once completely awake. For that exploring glance that the stranger had cast around the room had not been merely to survey the saloon, it had been in quest of a face, and when his eye had lighted on Jigger, he had come in at once.

But what could Jigger be to him?

Jigger had never seen him before. In the great spaces of his memory, where faces appeared more thickly than whirling leaves, never once had he laid eyes on either of the pair. The first man was tall, meager, with a crooked neck and a projecting Adam's apple. The skin was fitted tightly over the bones of his face. His hair was blond, his eyebrows very white, and his skin sun-blackened. It was altogether a face that would not be forgotten easily. The second fellow was an opposite type—fat, dark, with immense power swelling the shoulders and sleeves of his shirt.

The two looked perfectly the parts of cowpunchers; certainly they had spent their lives in the open, and there was nothing to catch the eyes about them as extraordinary except that both wore their guns well down the thigh, so that the handles of them were conveniently in grasp of the fingertips.

Having spent half a second glancing at them, Jigger spent the next moments in carefully analyzing the two. Certainly he never had seen their faces. He never had heard their names— from their talk he learned that the tall fellow was Tim and the shorter man was called Buzz. They looked the part of cowpunchers, perfectly, except that the palms of their hands did not seem to be thickened or calloused.

What could they want with Jigger unless they had been sent in to the town of Tucker Flat in order to locate Jigger and relay to him orders from Doc Landy?

Several more men came into the saloon. But it was apparent that they had nothing to do with the first couple. However, a few moments later both Buzz and Tim were seated at a table with two more. By the very way that tall Tim shuffled the cards, it was clear to Jigger that these fellows probably had easier ways of making money than working for it.

Hands uncalloused, guns worn efficiently though uncomfortably low, these were small indications, but they were enough to make Jigger suspicious. The two looked to him more and more like a couple of Landy's lawbreakers.

"How about you, stranger?" said Tim, nodding at Jigger. "Make a fifth at poker?"

"I've only got a few bucks on me," said Jigger. "But I'll sit in if you want."

He could have sworn that this game had been arranged by Tim and Buzz solely for the purpose of drawing him into it. And yet everything had been done very naturally.

He remained out for the first three hands, then on three queens he pulled in a jackpot. Half an hour later he was betting his last penny. He lost it at once.

"You got a nice spot of bad luck," said Buzz Mahoney, who was mixing the cards at the moment. "But stick with the game. If you're busted, we'll lend you something."

"I've got nothing worth a loan," said Jigger.

"Haven't you got a gun tucked away somewhere?"

"No. No gun."

And he saw a thin gleam of wonder and satisfaction commingled in the eyes of Tim Riley.

"Empty out your pockets," said Tim. "Maybe you've got a picture of your best girl. I'll lend you something on that."

He laughed as he spoke. They all laughed. And Jigger obediently put the contents of his pockets on the table, a jumble of odds and ends.

"All right," said Tim at once. "Lend you ten bucks on that, brother."

Ten dollars? The whole lot was not worth five, new. But Jigger accepted the money. He accepted and lost it all by an apparently foolish bet in the next hand. But he wanted to test the strangers at once.

"I'm through, boys," he said, and pushed back his chair.

He was eager to see if they would still persuade him to remain in the game. But not a word was said, except that Buzz Mahoney muttered: "Your bad luck is a regular long streak, today. Sorry to lose you, kid."

Jigger laughed a little, pushing in his cards with a hand that lingered on them for just an instant.

In that moment he had found what he expected—a little, almost microscopic smudge that was not quite true to the regular pattern on the backs of the cards. It was a tiny thing, but the eye of Jigger was a little sharper than that of a hawk that turns its head in the middle sky and sees in the dim forest of the grass below the scamper of a little field mouse.

The cards were marked. Mahoney or Tim Riley had done that. They were marked for the distinct purpose of beating Jigger, for the definite end of getting away something that had been in his possession. What was it that they had wanted so much? What was it that had brought them on his trail?

II

It was pitch dark when Doc Landy reached the deserted shack outside the town of Tucker Flat. He whistled once and again, and, when he received no answer, he began to curse heavily. In the darkness, with the swift surety of long practice, he stripped the packs from the mules, hobbled and side-lined them, and presently they were sucking up water noisily at the little rivulet that crossed the clearing.

The peddler, in the meantime, had kindled a small fire in the open fireplace that stood before the shack and he soon had the flames rising, as he laid out his cooking pans and provisions. This light struck upward only on his long jaw and heavy nose, merely glinting across the baldness of his head and the silver pockmarks that were littered over his features. When he turned, reaching here or there with his long arms, the huge, deformed bunch behind his shoulders loomed. It was rather a camel's hump of strength than a deformity of the spine.

Bacon began to hiss in the pan. Coffee bubbled in the pot. Potatoes were browning in the coals beside the fire. Soft pone steamed in its baking pan, and now the peddler set out a tin of plum jam and prepared to begin his feast.

It was at this moment that he heard a yawn, or what seemed a yawn, on the farther side of the clearing. The big hands of the peddler instantly were holding a shotgun in readiness. Peering through the shadows, on the very margin of his firelight he made out a dim patch of gold, then the glow of big eyes. At last he was aware of a big horse lying motionless on the ground while close to him, his head and shoulders comfortably pillowed on a hummock, appeared Jigger.

"Jigger!" yelled the peddler. "You been here all the time? Didn't you hear me whistle?"

"Why should I show up before eating time?" asked Jigger. He stood up and stretched himself. The stallion began to rise, also, but a gesture from the master made it sink to the ground again.

"I dunno why I should feed a gent too lazy to help me take off those packs and cook the meal," growled Doc Landy. And he thrust out his jaw in an excess of malice.

"You want to feed me because you always feed the hungry," said Jigger. "Because the bigness of old Doc's heart is one of the things that everyone talks about. A rough diamond, but a heart of gold. A . . ."

"The devil with the people and you, too," Doc said.

He looked on gloomily while Jigger, uninvited, helped himself to food and commenced to eat.

"Nothing but brown sugar for this coffee?" demanded Jigger.

"It's too good for you, even that way," answered Doc. "What makes you so hungry?"

"Because I didn't eat since noon."

"Why not? There's all the food in the world in Tucker Flat."

"Broke," said Jigger.

"Broke? How can you be broke when I gave you fifteen hundred dollars two weeks ago?" shouted Doc.

"Well," said Jigger, "the fact is that faro parted me from five hundred."

"Faro? You fool!" said Doc. "But that still left a whole thousand . . . and from the looks of you, you didn't spend anything on clothes."

"I ran into Jeff Beacon, and old Jeff was flat."

"How much did you give him?"

"I don't know. I gave him the roll, and he took a part of it."

"You don't know how much?"

"I forgot to count it, afterward."

"Are you clean crazy, Jigger?"

"Jeff needed money worse than I did. A man with a family to take care of needs a lot of money, Doc."

"Still, that left you several hundred. What happened to it?"

"I met Steve Walters when he was feeling lucky and I staked him for poker."

"What did his luck turn into?"

"Wonderful, Doc. He piled up nearly two thousand, in an hour."

"Where was your share of it?"

"Why, Steve hit three bad hands and plunged, and he was taken to the cleaners. So I gave him something to eat on and rode away." Jigger paused, then added: "And when today came along, somehow I had only a few dollars in my pocket."

"I'd rather pour water on the desert than put

money in your pocket!" shouted Doc Landy. "It ain't human, the way you throw it away."

He continued to glare for a moment, and growl. He was still shaking his head as he commenced champing his food.

"You didn't even have the price of a meal?" he demanded at last.

"That's quite a story."

"I don't want to hear it," snapped Doc Landy. "I've got a job for you."

"I've just finished a job for you," said Jigger.

"What of it?" demanded Doc Landy. "You signed up to do what I pleased for three months, didn't you?"

"I did." Jigger sighed. He thought regretfully of the impulse that had led him into putting himself at the beck and call of this old vulture. But his word had been given.

"And there's more than two months of that time left, ain't there?"

"I suppose so."

"Then listen to me, while I tell you what I want you to do."

"Wait till you hear my story."

"Rats with your story. I don't want to hear it."

"Oh, you'll want to hear it all right."

"What makes you think so?" asked the peddler.

"Because you like one thing even more than money."

"What do I like more?"

"Trouble," said Jigger. "You love it like the rat that you are."

In fact, as the peddler thrust out his jaw and wrinkled his eyes he looked very like a vast rodent. He overlooked the insult to ask: "What sort of trouble?"

"Something queer. I told you I was broke today. That's because I lost my last few dollars playing poker. I played the poker because I *wanted* to lose."

"Wanted to?" echoed Doc Landy. "That's too crazy even for you. I don't believe it."

"I'll tell you how it was. I was sitting with a glass of beer when two *hombres* walked into the saloon . . . by the look they gave me, I knew they were on my trail . . . and I wondered why, because I'd never seen them before. I let them get me into a poker game and take my cash. I knew that wasn't what they wanted. When I was frozen out, they were keen to lend me a stake and got me to empty my pockets on the table. I put a handful of junk on the table, then they loaned me ten dollars, and I let that go in the next hand. They didn't offer to stake me again. They wanted something that was in my pockets. When they got that, they were satisfied. Now, then, what was it that they were after?"

"What did they look like?" asked Doc Landy.

"Anything up to murder," said Jigger promptly.

"What was the stuff you put on the table?"

"Half a pack of wheat-straw papers, a full sack of tobacco, a penknife with one blade broken, a twist of twine, sulphur matches, a leather wallet with nothing in it except a letter from a girl, a key ring and some keys, a handkerchief, a pocket comb in a leather case, a stub of a pencil. That was all."

"The letter from the girl. What girl?" asked Landy.

"None of your business," said Jigger.

"It may have been *their* business, though."

"Not likely. Her name wasn't signed to the letter, anyway. She didn't say anything except talk about the weather. Nobody could have made anything of that letter."

"Any marks on the wallet?"

"None that mattered, so far as I know."

"I've seen you write notes on cigarette papers."

"No notes on those."

"What were you doing with a key ring and keys? You don't own anything with locks on it."

"Caught my eye in the pawnshop today. Little silver snake with green eyes."

"Anything queer about that snake?"

"Good Mexican work. That's all."

"The letter's the answer," said Doc Landy. "There was something in that letter."

"They're welcome to it."

"Or in the keys. What sort of keys?"

"Three for padlocks, two regular door keys,

something that looked like a skeleton, and a little flat key of white metal."

"Any marks on those keys?"

"Only on the little one. The number on it was one-two-six-five."

"You've got an eye," said Doc Landy. "When I think what an eye and a brain and a hand you've got, it sort of makes me sick. Nothing in the world that you couldn't do if you weren't so dog-gone' honest."

Jigger did not answer. He was brooding, and now he said: "Could it have been the keys? I didn't think of that." Then he added: "It *was* the keys!"

"How d'you know?" asked Doc.

"I remember now that when I bought them, the pawnbroker said that he had just put the ring out for sale a couple of hours before."

"Ha!" grunted Doc. "You mean that the two gents had gone back to the pawnshop to redeem the key ring?"

"Why not? Maybe they'd come a long way to redeem that key ring. Maybe the time was up yesterday. They found the thing gone . . . they got my description . . . they trailed me . . . they worked the stuff out of my pockets onto the table . . . and there you are. Doc, they were headed for some sort of dirty work . . . something big."

Doc Landy began to sweat. He forgot to drink his coffee. "We'll forget the other job I was going to give you," he said. "Maybe there ain't a bean in this, but we'll run it down."

"I knew you'd smell the poison in the air and like it," said Jigger, grinning.

"What would put you on their trail? What would the number on that little key mean?"

"Hotel room? No, it wasn't big enough for that. It couldn't mean anything in this part of the world . . . except a post-office box. No other lock would be shallow enough for it to fit."

"There's an idea!" exclaimed Doc Landy. "That's a big number . . . one-two-six-five. Take a big town to have that many post-office boxes."

"Weldon is the only town big enough for that . . . the only town inside of three hundred miles."

"That pair is traveling for Weldon," agreed Landy. "They wanted that bunch of keys. Get 'em, Jigger! That's your job. Just get those keys and find out what they're to open. And start now."

III

Buzz Mahoney, opening the door of his room at the hotel in Tucker Flat, lit a match to ignite the lamp on the center table. Then he heard a whisper behind him and tried to turn around, but a blow landed accurately at the base of his skull and dropped him down a well of darkness. Jigger, leaning over him, unhurried, lit another match, and, fumbling through the pockets, found almost at once the silver snake key ring. Then he descended to the street, using a back window instead of the lobby and the front door. Before he had gone half a block, he heard stamping and shouting in the hotel, and knew that his victim had recovered and was trying to discover the source of his fall.

Jigger, pausing near the first streak of lamplight that shone through a window, examined the keys with a swift glance.

There had been seven keys before; there were only six, now. That was what sent Jigger swiftly around the corner to the place where Doc Landy waited for him.

"I've got them," he said, "but the one for the post-office box is gone. Mahoney had the rest, but Tim Riley is gone with the little key."

"There's something in that post-office box," answered Doc. "Go and get it."

"He's got a good head start," answered Jigger.

"He's got a good start, but you've got your horse, and if Fanfare can't make up the lost ground, nothing can. Ride for Weldon and try to catch Tim Riley on the way. I'm heading straight on for Weldon myself. I'll get there sometime tomorrow. Quit the trails and head straight for Weldon Pass. You'll catch your bird there."

Jigger sat on his heels and closed his eyes. He was seeing in his mind all the details of the ground over which he would have to travel, if he wished to take a short cut to Weldon Pass. Then he stood up, nodded, stretched again.

"I'll run along," he said.

"Have another spot of money?" asked the peddler. He took out $50, counted it with a grudging hand from his wallet, and passed it to Jigger, who received it without thanks.

"How long before somebody cuts your gizzard open to get your money, Doc?" he asked.

"That's what salts the meat and makes the game worthwhile," said Doc Landy. "Never knowing whether I'm gonna wake up when I go to sleep at night."

"How many murders do you dream about, Doc?" pursued Jigger casually.

"I got enough people in my dreams," said Doc Landy, grinning. "And some of 'em keep on talking after I know they're dead. But my conscience don't bother me none. I ain't such a fool, Jigger."

Jigger turned on his heel without answer or farewell. Five minutes later he was traveling toward Weldon Pass on the back of the stallion.

If Tim Riley had in fact started so long ahead of him toward the town of Weldon, it would take brisk travel to catch him in the narrow throat of the pass, so Jigger laid out an air line and traveled it as straight as a bird. There were ups and downs that ordinary men on ordinary horses never would have attempted. Jigger was on his feet half the time, climbing rugged slopes up which the stallion followed him like a great cat, or again Jigger worked his way down some perilous steep with the golden horse scampering and sliding to the rear, always with his nose close to the ground to study the exact places where his master had stepped. For the man knew exactly what the horse could do, and never took him over places too slippery or too abrupt for him to cover. In this work they gave the impression of two friends struggling toward a common end, rather than master and servant.

So they came out on a height above Weldon Pass, and, looking down it, Jigger saw the moon break through clouds and gild the pass with light. It was a wild place, with scatterings of hardy brush here and there, even an occasional tree, but on the whole it looked like a junk heap of stone with a course kicked through the center of it. Rain had been falling recently. The whole pass was bright with water, and it was against the thin gleam of this background that Jigger saw the small shadow of the other rider coming toward him. He went down the last abrupt slope at once to intercept the course of the other rider.

He was hardly at the bottom before he could hear the faint clinking sounds made by the hoofs of the approaching horse. A whisper made the stallion sink from view behind some small boulders. Jigger himself ran up to the top of a boulder half the size of a house and crouched there. He could see the stranger coming, the head of the horse nodding up and down in the pale moonlight. Jigger tied a bandanna around the lower part of his face.

Ten steps from Jigger's waiting place, he made sure that it was tall Tim Riley in person, for there Riley stopped his horse and let it drink from a little freshet that ran across the narrow floor of the ravine. It was a magnificent horse that he rode—over sixteen hands, sloping shoulders, high withers, big bones, well let-down hocks, and flat knees. *A horse too good for a working cowpuncher to have,* thought Jigger. And his last doubt about the character of Tim Riley disappeared. The man was a crooked card player with a crooked companion; he was probably a criminal in other ways, as well. Men are not apt to make honest journeys through the middle of the night and over places as wild as the Weldon Pass.

When the horse had finished drinking, Riley rode on again. He was passing the boulder that sheltered Jigger when his mount stopped suddenly and threw up its head with a snort. Riley, with the speed of an automatic reaction, snatched out a gun. There was a well-oiled ease in the movement, a professional touch of grace that did not escape the eye of Jigger. He could only take his man half by surprise, now, but he rose from behind his rampart of rock and leaped, headlong.

He sprang from behind, yet the flying shadow of danger seemed to pass over the brain of Riley. He jerked his head and gun around while Jigger was still in the air, then Jigger struck him with the full lunging weight of his body, and they rolled together from the back of the horse.

The gun had exploded once while they were in the air. Jigger remained unscathed, and now he found himself fighting for his life against an enemy as strong and swift and fierce as a mountain lion.

A hundred times Jigger had fought with his hands, but always victory had been easy. The ancient science of jiujitsu, which he had spent patient years learning, gave him a vast advantage in spite of his slender bulk. He had struggled with great two hundred pounders who were hardened fighting men, but always it was like the battle between the meager wasp and the huge powerful tarantula. The spider fights with blind strength, laying hold with its steel shears wherever it can; the wasp drives its poisoned sting at the nerve centers.

And that is the art of jiujitsu. At the pits of the arms or the side of the neck or the back, or inside the legs or in the pit of the stomach, there are places where the great nerves come close to the surface, vulnerable to a hard pressure or a sharp blow. And Jigger knew those spots as an anatomist might know them. Men who fought him were rarely hurt unless they hurled their own weight at him too blindly, for half the great art of jiujitsu lies in using the strength of the antagonist against him. Usually the victim of Jigger recovered as from a trance, with certain vaguely tingling pains still coursing through parts of his body. But not a bone would be broken, and the bruises were few.

He tried all his art now, and he found that art checked and baffled at every turn. Tall and spare of body, Tim Riley looked almost fragile, but from the first touch Jigger found him a creature of whalebone and Indian rubber. Every fiber of Riley's body was a strong wire, and in addition he was an expert wrestler. Before they had rolled twice on the ground, Jigger was struggling desperately in the defense.

Then the arm of Riley caught him with a frightful stranglehold that threatened to break his neck before it choked him. Suddenly Jigger lay still.

Tim Riley seemed to sense surrender in this yielding, this sudden pulpiness of body and muscle. Instead of offering quarter, Riley began to snarl like a dog that has sunk its teeth in a death grip. He kept jerking the crook of his arm deeper and deeper into the throat of Jigger, who lay inert, face down. Flames and smoke seemed to shoot upward through Jigger's brain, but in that instant of relaxation he had gathered his strength and decided on his counterstroke.

He twisted his right leg outside that of his enemy, raised the foot until with his heel he located the knee of Riley, then kicked the sharp heel heavily against the inside of the joint.

Tim Riley yelled with agony. The blow fell again, and he twisted his body frantically away from the torture. That movement gave Jigger his chance and with the sharp edge of his palm, hardened almost like wood by long practice in the trick, he struck the upper arm of Riley.

It loosened its grip like a numb, dead thing. With his other arm Riley tried to get the same fatal hold, but Jigger had twisted like a writhing snake. He struck again with the edge of the palm, and the blow fell like the stroke of a blunt cleaver across the million nerves that run up the side of the neck. The head of Riley fell over as though an axe had struck deep. He lay not motionless but vaguely stirring, making a groaning, wordless complaint.

Jigger, in a moment, had trussed him like a bird for market. Still the wits had not fully returned to Riley as Jigger rifled his pocket. But he found not a sign of the little flat white key that had the number 1265 stamped upon it.

He crumpled the clothes of the man, feeling that such a small object might have been hidden in a seam, then he pulled off the boots of Riley and when he took out the first insole, he found what he wanted. The little key flashed like an eye in the moonlight, then he dropped it into his pocket.

The voice of Tim Riley pleaded from the ground: "You ain't gonna leave me here, brother, are you? And what on earth did you use to hit me? Where did you have it, up your sleeve?"

Jigger leaned and looked into the lean, hard face of the other. Then he muttered: "You'll be all right. People will be riding through the pass in the early morning. So long, partner."

Then he took the horse of Riley by the reins and led it away among the rocks toward the place where he had left Fanfare, the stallion.

IV

Neither on the streets of Weldon nor in the post office itself did people pay much attention to Jigger because the Weldon newspaper had published an extra that told that the body of Joe Mendoza, the escaped fugitive from the state prison, had been found. That news was of sufficient importance to occupy all eyes with reading and all tongues with talk, but all it meant to Jigger was the cover under which he could approach his work.

He went straight into the post office and found there what he had expected in a town of the size of Weldon—a whole wall filled by the little mailboxes, each with a glass insert in the door so that it could be seen if mail were waiting inside.

And in the right-hand corner, shoulder-high, appeared Number 1265. Inside it, he could see a single thin envelope.

The key fitted at once; the little bolt of the lock slipped with a click, and the door opened. Jigger took out the envelope and slammed the small door so that the spring lock engaged.

On the envelope was written: *Mr. Oliver Badget, Box 1265, Weldon.* And in the upper left-hand corner: *To be delivered only to Oliver Badget in person.*

The camping places of the peddler in his tours through the mountains were perfectly known to Jigger. Therefore he was waiting in a wooded hollow just outside of Weldon when Doc Landy shambled into the glade late that afternoon.

Doc Landy shouted an excited greeting, but Jigger remained flat on his back, his hands cupped under his head while he stared up through the green gloom of a pine tree at the little splashes of blue heaven above. The sun in slanted patches warmed his body.

But the peddler, not waiting to pull the pack saddles off his tired mules, stood over Jigger and stared critically down at him.

"That gent Riley was a tough *hombre*, eh? Too tough for you, Jigger?" he asked.

"I got the key from him," said Jigger. "There was a box numbered one-two-six-five at the post office, and this was what was inside."

He fished the envelope from his pocket and tossed it into the air. The big hand of the peddler darted out and caught the prize. Jerking out the fold of paper that it contained, Doc Landy stared at a singular pattern. There was not a written word on the soiled sheet. There was only a queer jumble of dots, triangles, and one wavering, crooked line that ran across the paper from one corner to the other. Beside one bend of the wavering line appeared a cross.

"This here is the spot," argued the peddler.

"The cross is the spot," agreed Jigger. "And a lot that means?"

"The triangles are trees," said Doc.

"Or mountains," answered Jigger.

"The dots . . . what would they be, kid?"

"How do I know? Cactus . . . rocks . . . I don't know."

"This crooked line is a road, Jigger."

"Or a valley, or a ravine."

"It's hell," said Landy.

He stared at Jigger, who remained motionless.

The wind ruffled his black hair; the blue of his eyes was as still and peaceful as the sky above them. Doc Landy cursed again, and then sat down, cross-legged.

"Put your brain on this here, Jigger," he said. "Two brains are better than one."

"I've put my brain on it, but you can see for yourself that we'll never make anything out of it."

"Why not?"

"Well, it's simply a chart to stir up the memory of Oliver Badget. Oliver is the boy who knows what those marks mean. Call it a road . . . that crooked line. Well, at the seventh bend from the lower corner of the page, there, along that road, there's something planted. Oliver wants to be able to find it. But where does the road begin? Where does he begin to count the bends?"

"From Weldon," suggested the peddler.

"Yes. Or from a bridge, or a clump of trees, or something like that. And there's twenty roads or trails leading into Weldon."

Doc Landy groaned. He took out a plug of chewing tobacco, clamped his teeth into a corner of it, and bit off a liberal quid with a single powerful closing of his jaws. He began to masticate the tobacco slowly.

"A gent with something on hand wants to put it away," he said, thinking aloud. "He takes and hides it. He hides it in a place so dog-gone' mixed up that even he can't be sure that he'll remember. So he leaves a chart. Where's he going to hide the *chart,* though?"

"Where nobody would ever think of looking," agreed Jigger. "He rents a post-office box and puts the chart in an envelope addressed to himself. Nobody else could get that envelope because nobody else has the key, and nobody could call for mail in Badget's name and get the envelope, either. Because that letter would have to be signed for in Badget's signature before the clerk would turn the thing over. But now that he's got the chart hidden, all he has to do is to hide the key. And where would he hide the key? Well, in a place just as public as the post-office box, where everybody could see it. So he hocks that key ring and all the keys on it at a pawnshop."

Landy sighed. "Nobody would go to all of this trouble, Jigger," he commented, "unless what was hidden out was a dog-gone' big pile."

"Nobody would," agreed Jigger.

"And now Mister Badget turns up and tries to get his key and finds that his time has just run out. He hurries like the devil to get to that key in time, but he's too late. Jigger has the key. He gets it away from Jigger. . . . Why, that all sounds dog-gone' reasonable and logical."

"Badget isn't another name for Riley or for Mahoney," declared Jigger.

"Why not?"

"Well, Badget himself could go to the post office without the key and get the letter any time by signing for it."

"True," agreed Landy. Then he added, after a moment of thought: "Badget couldn't come himself. He had to send friends to make sure that that key didn't get into the wrong hands. He sent friends to maybe just pay the interest due on the pawnbroker's loan and renew it, and pay for the post-office box. Why didn't Badget come himself? Sick? In jail?"

"Or dead," said Jigger.

"Jigger, there's something important hidden out where that cross is marked."

"We'll never find it without a key to the chart," said Jigger. "It's a good little map, all right, but unless we know what part of the country to fit it to, we'll never locate what's under the cross. It may be a district five hundred miles from here, for all we know."

"What'll we do?" asked Doc Landy.

"Wait, Doc. That's the only good thing that we can do."

"What good will waiting do?"

"The postmaster has a master key for all of those boxes. Well, the postmaster is going to lose that key today or tomorrow. And right afterward, Box One-Two-Six-Five is going to be opened."

"There won't be anything in it," protested Landy. "Whatcha mean, Jigger?"

"You can copy the chart, and then I'll put the original back in the post-office box."

"What happens then? You mean that Riley and Mahoney come along, rob the postmaster of the master key, get the chart, and then start out on the trail with us behind them?"

"With me behind them," corrected Jigger. "I don't need you."

The big peddler swore. "Yeah," he said, "you can disappear like a sand flea and turn up like a wildcat whenever you want to. You'll be able to trail 'em, all right."

Jigger sighed. "Copy the chart," he said. "I'm going to sleep. Because after I take that envelope back to the post office, I've got to find a place and stay awake day and night to see who goes into that building, and who comes out again."

Landy, without a word of answer, sat down to his drawing.

V

There was a three-story hotel opposite the post office, and here Jigger lay at a window night and day for four long days. They were hot, windless days, and he hardly closed his eyes for more than a half hour at a time, but the keenness of his attention never diminished. Over the low shoulders of the post office, from his place of vantage, he could look all around the environs of the building he spied upon. The nights were clear, with moonlight. The days were the more difficult. Because he could not tell when Riley or Mahoney would appear in one of the sudden swirls of people who slipped suddenly through the swing doors of the building, disappeared, and came out again a few moments later.

It was quite possible that they would attempt to disguise themselves. But even then he would have more than a good chance of identifying them. He had learned long ago to look not only at the face of a man but also at the shape of his head, the angle of nose and forehead, and particularly at any strangeness of contour in the ear. A man may become either thin or fat, but his height is not altered. And the general outline of the head and shoulders, whether the man comes toward the eye or goes from it, may often be recognized.

Even so, hawk-eyed as he was, it would be fumbling in the dark—and like a patient fisher he remained waiting. Agonies of impatience he hid away behind a smile.

One cause of his impatience was his desire to finish up the job for Landy. Doc had helped him in his great need but had expected a three months' servitude in exchange. Jigger loved danger, and Doc could supply it, but it was unsavory, unclean, and Jigger liked things as shining clear as the coat of the stallion, Fanfare. But his code made him live up to his given word. What he would do to Doc when his term of service was up put the only good taste in his mouth in many a day.

It was on the fourth day that tall Doc Landy stalked into the room and pushed his dusty hat back on his head. The hot reek of the outdoors entered with him.

He said: "Oliver Badget was Joe Mendoza. I just seen a bit of Mendoza's handwriting, so I know. Buzz Mahoney and Tim Riley were the best friends of Joe. Mendoza is dead. Buzz and Tim are carrying on where Mendoza left off. That means they're starting something big. So big, that Mendoza risked his neck to get out of prison. He must've met those two *hombres*. Before he died, he told them things. And it's my idea, Jigger, that what that chart tells is the location of the cache where Mendoza put away the whole savings of his life."

The teeth of Landy clicked together. His eyes grew green with bright greed. "And Mendoza never spent nothing. He never did nothing but save," he added. "Jigger, I've got three of my best men, and they're gonna ride with you when you start the game."

"I work a lone hand or I don't work at all," said Jigger dreamily as he lay stretched on his bed, peering steadily out the window.

"Damn it," growled Landy, "if you try to handle

270

the two of 'em, they'll sure bust you full of lead. Mendoza never had nothing to do with gents that wasn't murderers. Those are two gunmen, Jigger, and when you handled 'em before, you was dealing with rattlers without knowing it."

"I'll handle 'em alone or not at all," said Jigger in the same voice.

"Jigger . . . you'll carry a gun, then, won't you?"

Jigger shook his head. "Any fool can carry a gun," he answered. "The fun of the game is handling fire with your bare hands."

There was a muffled, snarling sound from Doc Landy. Then he strode from the room without another word.

And five minutes later Jigger shuddered. For a man with a long linen duster on had just stepped through the front door of the post office. The duster covered him very efficiently, but a certain weight about the shoulders, a certain sense of power in the arms was not lost on Jigger.

He was off his bed, down the stairs, and instantly in the stable behind the hotel. A moment later he had jerked the saddle on the back of the stallion and snapped the bridle over his head. Then he hurried down the alley and crossed into the vacant lot beside the hotel where a clump of tall shrubs covered him. He could see without being seen.

And he had hardly taken his post before the

man in the linen duster came out from the post office again, paused to yawn widely, glanced up and down the street with quick eyes, and turned the corner.

Jigger, running to the same corner, had a glimpse of two men swinging on the backs of two fine horses. At once the pair swung away at a rapid canter.

They left Weldon, headed north for five miles, swung sharply to the west, then went straight south through the mountains.

For two days, Jigger shivered in the wet winds and the whipping rains of the high ravines, following his quarry.

It was close work, dangerous work. Sometimes in a naked valley he had to let the pair get clear out of sight before he ventured to take the trail again. Once, coming through a dense fog that was simply a cloud entangled in the heights, he came suddenly around a rock, face to face, with a starry light. And through the mist, not five steps away, he heard the loud voice of Buzz Mahoney yell out: "Who's there? What's that?"

"A mountain sheep, you fool," suggested Tim Riley.

Six days out of Weldon, Jigger was riding anxiously through a ravine that was cluttered with such a litter of rocks that danger might have hidden there in the form of whole regiments. It was only the hair-trigger sensitiveness of the nose of the stallion that detected trouble ahead.

He stopped, jerked up his head, and the next instant Jigger saw the wavering of sunlight on a bit of steel, the blue brightness of a leveled gun.

He whirled Fanfare away. Two rifles barked, sent long, clanging echoes down the ravine, and Jigger swayed slowly out from the saddle, dropped, and hung head down with trailing arms, his right leg hooked over the saddle as though caught in the stirrup leather and so, precariously, supported.

The rifles spoke no more.

Instead, two riders began to clatter furiously in pursuit. A good mile they rushed their swift horses along, but Fanfare, with his master still hanging at his side, widened the distance of his lead with every stride and finally was lost to view among the sea of boulders.

After that, the noise of the pursuit no longer beat through the ravine, and Jigger pulled himself back into the saddle. His leg ached as though the bone had been broken, his head spun, but there was no real harm done by his maneuver.

He turned again on the trail. All that Doc Landy had told him, all that he could have guessed, was reinforced doubly now. For when men would not delay to capture such a horse as Fanfare when the rider was apparently wounded to death, it was sure proof that Mahoney and Riley were bound toward a great goal.

They went on securely, now, but steadily. They cleft through the mountains, following the high Lister Pass, and then they dipped down along the side of the range into the terrible sun mist and dusty glare of Alkali Flat.

Imagine a bowl a hundred miles across, rimmed with cool blue distance on either side but paved with white heat and the welter and dance of the reflected sun. That was Alkali Flat.

Jigger, looking from the rim of the terrible depression, groaned softly. He glanced up and saw three soaring buzzards come over the head of the mountain, turn, and sweep with untroubled wings back the way they had come. Even at that height, they seemed to dread the pungent heat that poured up from the vast hollow.

Jigger, sitting in the shadow of a rock, sat down to think. He could find no resource in his mind. There was no way in which he could travel out into the desert.

Whoever had chosen to hide a treasure in the midst of such an ocean of despair had chosen well.

In the middle of the day, a man needed three pints of water an hour. A fellow whose canteen went dry in the middle of that hell would be mad with thirst by the time he had walked fifteen miles, at the most. They went mad and died—every man the same way. The first act was to tear off the shirt. The second was to commence digging with bare hands in the sand and the rocks. They would be found that way afterward, the nails broken from their fingers, the flesh tattered, the very bones at the tips of the fingers splintered by the frightful, blind efforts of the dying men.

Jigger, remembering one dreadful picture he had seen, slowly ran the pink tip of his tongue across his lips and sat up to breathe more easily. He had a canteen that would hold a single quart—and the valley was a hundred miles across!

He had saddlebags, of course. They were new and strong, of the heaviest canvas.

He took a pair of them and went to the nearest sound of running water. He drank and drank again of that delightfully bubbling spring—the mere sight of Alkali Flat had implanted in him an insatiable thirst. Then he filled one of the bags. The canvas was perfectly water-tight, but the seams let the water spurt out in streams.

He looked about him, not in despair, but with the sense of one condemned. If he could not enter the desert assured of a fair chance of getting through, why, he would enter it without that chance and trust to luck like a madman.

He was drawn by that perverse hunger for danger like a dizzy man by the terrible edge of a cliff.

Then he saw the pine trees that were filling the mountain air with sweetness, and he remembered their resin.

Resin? It exuded from them in little fresh runs; it dripped from the wounded bark; it flavored the air with its clean scent. He began to collect it rapidly, with his knife, and, as he got it, he commenced to smear the stuff over the seams of his saddlebags, which he turned inside out.

He had two pairs, and he resined all four in hardly more than an hour. That was why the stallion was well weighted down with a load of the purest spring water, going down the slope toward Alkali Flat.

His master went ahead of him, jauntily, whistling a little, but the heat from the desert already was beginning to sting the eyes and make the lids of them tender.

VI

In Alkali Flat, the earth was not a mother. It was a grave. Once there had been a river running through it; now there was only the hollow trough filled with the dead bones of the stream. Once there had been trees; now there were only the scarecrow trunks of a few ancient survivors. It was worse than the Sahara, because in the Sahara there was never life and here there was a ghost of it.

As Jigger passed down into the frightful glare of that wasted land, he saw the trail of Mahoney and Tim Riley lead up to the bank of the dead river and then pass down the length of it. He felt that he knew, at once, the nature of the windings that had been depicted on the chart and he could not help admiring the cleverness of Joe Mendoza, leaving his treasure here in the middle of a salt waste.

The temperature was above a hundred.

That is a phrase that people use casually, liberally without understanding. Actually every part of a degree above blood heat begins to draw the strength from the heart. A dry heat is then an advantage in a sense, because the quick evaporation of the perspiration cools the flesh a little.

But the heat in the great Alkali Flat was above a hundred and twenty. There were twenty-two degrees of fatal heat, and the dryness not merely turned sweat into mist at once it laid hold on the flesh like a thousand leeches, sucking out the liquid from the body.

The feet of Jigger began to burn in his boots. There seemed to be sand under his eyelids. The drying lips threatened to crack wide open. And thirst blew down his throat like a dusty wind at every breath he drew.

At the same time, the skin of his face commenced to pull and contract, and the dry skin of his body was rubbed and chafed by his clothes.

Fanfare, indomitable in all conditions, now

held on his way with his ears laid flat against his skull.

When Jigger looked up, he saw a wedge of three buzzards sliding out from the mountain height and hanging in the air. They might shun the air above the horrible flat, but not when foolish living creatures attempted to cross the floor of the oven.

What insane beings, even a Mahoney and a Riley, ventured on such a journey by the light of the day?

Jigger looked from the dizzy sky back to the earth. It was like a kitchen yard, a yard on which thousands of gallons of soapy water, in the course of generations, have been flung upon a summer-baked soil, thrice a day. For a singular odor rose from the ground. And it was everywhere gray-white.

Along the banks of the river one could see where water had once flowed at varying levels. The banks had been eaten back by the now-dead stream. Here and there, at the edges of the levels, appeared the dry roots of long-vanished plants and trees, as fine as hair.

There was no steady breeze, but now and again a twist of the air sucked up dust in a small air pool that moved with swiftness for a short distance and then melted away. If one of those white phantoms swayed toward Jigger, he swerved the horse to avoid it. Fanfare himself shrank from the contact, for the alkali dust burned the passages of nose and lungs and mouth like dry lye and the eyes were eaten by that unslaked lime.

Yet the other pair still advanced more deeply into that fire. An hour went by, and another, and another, and another. At a walk or a dog-trot, Fanfare stuck to his work. His coat was beginning to stare as his sweat dried and the salt of the perspiration stiffened the gloss of his hair. When Jigger stroked the glorious neck of the horse, a thin dust followed his hand.

They had passed the danger point, long ago. That is to say, they had passed the point when a man could safely attempt to journey out of the alkali hell without water to carry. A fellow with a two-quart canteen, no matter how he nursed it, would probably be frantic for liquid before he reached the promise of the mountains that, already, were turning brown and blue in the distance.

And then the two figures far ahead, only discernible in the spyglass that Jigger now and then used for spotting them, dipped away from the flat and disappeared. They had descended into the stream bed.

It might mean that they had spotted the pursuer and were going to stalk him in ambush. It might mean, also, that they had reached the proper bend of the dry draw and that they were about to search for the marked spot on the chart.

Jigger, taking a chance on the second possibility, pushed Fanfare ahead rapidly until he was close to the point of the disappearance. Conscience, duty, a strange spirit seemed to ride in his shadow and drive him ahead, but his conscious mind rebelled against this torment. It told him to rush away toward one of those spots of cool, blue mirage that continually wavered into view on the face of the desert; it told him that all was useless—wealth, fame, honor no more real than the welter of the heat waves. But he kept on.

When he was reasonably close, he dipped Fanfare down into the channel of the vanished river, and watered him from the second saddle-bag. The water was now almost the heat of blood and it had developed a foul taste from cooking inside the heavy canvas, but Fanfare supped up the water greedily until the bag was empty.

There remained to Jigger one half of his original supply, and yet one half of his labor had not been completed.

Under a steep of the bank where there was a fall of shadow, he placed the horse and made him lie down. But the shadow was not a great blessing. The dimness seemed to thicken the air; it was like breathing dust, and the sand, even under the shadow, was hot to the touch.

Here Fanfare was left, lifting his head and sending after his master a whinny of anxiety, no louder than a whisper. For the stallion knew as well as any man the reason those buzzards wheeled in the stillness of the hot air above.

Would the two men ahead take heed of the second group of the buzzards? Or would they fail to notice, earthbound as their eyes must be, that the vultures wheeled and sailed in two parts?

Jigger went on swiftly, but with care. And he could wish, now, that he had not left Weldon with empty hands. He had his knife, to be sure, and if he came to close range, that heavy knife with its needle-sharp point would be as deadly in his hands as any gun. It might well dispose of one of the pair, but the second one would certainly take revenge for his fall.

Very clearly Jigger knew what it meant if the couple were real companions of Joe Mendoza, that super murderer. He would have none about him except savages as brutal as wild beasts. He would have none except experts in slaughter.

This knowledge made the step of Jigger lighter than the step of a wildcat as he heard, directly around the next bend, the sound of blows sinking into the earth. From the sharp edge of the bank he saw, as he peered around it, both Mahoney and tall Tim Riley hard at work with a pick and a shovel that they had taken from their packs.

Their two horses, like the stallion, had been placed under the partial shadow of the western bank. One stood head down, like a dying thing; the other, with more of the invincible Western toughness supporting its knees and its spirit, wandered with slow steps down the draw, sniffing curiously at the strange dead roots that projected here and there from the bank.

The two workers, hard at it, had now opened a good-size hole in the earth and they were driving it deeper and deeper when Mahoney uttered a wild cry and flung both arms above his head. Then, leaning, he tore at something buried in the earth. There was the brittle noise of the rending of a tough fabric. Mahoney jerked up, holding what seemed a torn strip of tarpaulin in his hands, and leaned immediately to grasp it again. Riley helped him. They were both yelling out senseless, meaningless words.

And now Jigger saw a very strange thing to do, and did it. He slipped quietly out from his post of vantage and went up to the horse that was wandering with slow steps down the bank, the water sloshing with soft gurglings inside the burlap-wrapped huge canteen that hung from the saddle.

Jigger took the horse calmly by the bridle and led it, step by step, around the bend. He had the horse almost out of view when Mahoney, leaping to his feet, apparently looked straight at the thief. Instead of drawing a gun, Buzz Mahoney pulled off his hat and began to wave it and shout with delight. Tim Riley also commenced to prance around like a crazy man.

"The whole insides of the Levison Bank!" yelled Riley. "Kid, we got it! We're rich for life!"

They were blind with happiness. That was why Mahoney had failed to see the thief in his act of stealing, and now Jigger was walking steadily down the draw with the horse behind him. He kept on until he reached the great stallion, which rose eagerly to meet him and touch noses with the other horse.

Then Jigger mounted Fanfare and put two miles of steady cantering behind him. After that, he rode up the bank to the level of the ground above, and waited.

He sat in the shade under the side of Fanfare and ventured to smoke a cigarette that filled his lungs with a milder fire than that of the alkali dust.

One horse, two men, and the long, burning stretch of the desert to cross before the blue peace of the mountains surrounded them. It seemed to Jigger that there was nothing in the world so beautiful as mountains, these mountains to the north. Yes, perhaps there were other regions even more delightful. There were the great Arctic and Antarctic plains where the ice of ages is piled. But to lie all day where water can flow across the body, where the lips can draw up clear water every moment—that is a bliss beyond words.

It was easy to think, also, of the cool, shadowy interiors of saloons, and the refreshing pungency of beer. Barrels of beer buried in vast casks of chipped ice and snow.

Men of sense should work with ice. What happy fellows are those who deliver the great, white, ponderous cakes of it, sawing and splitting it up for customers, drifting comfortably from house to house.

Time passed. He watered the two horses and himself drank, sparingly. There was still plenty of sun. It was high, high above the horizon, and those two fellows who had found the treasure of Joe Mendoza did not seem, as yet, to have discovered the loss of the second horse with more than half of their remaining water supply.

Well, the wind of joy would cool them for a spell, but afterward. . . .

He thought, too, of the old, white-headed banker, Levison, still straight-backed, level-eyed, fearless of the hatred that men poured on him since the failure of his bank after the robbery.

What fools the officers of the law had been not to suspect that the job was that of Mendoza. Three men shot down wantonly. That was like Mendoza, and Riley and Mahoney were no doubt of the murderous crew that attended the chief on that day of the hold-up.

It all made a simple picture, now. Escaping with their spoil, Mendoza had attended to the

284

hiding of it. They would disappear from the face of the land for a time. Then, at an appointed date, they would re-gather.

But in the meantime, Mendoza had been captured on some other charge; he had been put into the prison, and, when he attempted to break out at the allotted moment, he had been shot. He had passed on his information, loyally, to his two men.

That was the story, and Jigger knew it as well as though he had heard it from the lips of the pair.

And now, at last, the two came up over the edge of the draw and started toward the mountains, one of them in the saddle, the other riding behind.

Jigger fell in behind them.

That terrible dryness of the air, that flaming of the sun no longer seemed hostile. It was performing his work.

At the end of a long, long hour, the mountains seemed even farther away than they had been at the beginning. And Jigger saw the pair halt. They took off the big canteen from the side of their horse, drank, and then appeared to be measuring out some of the liquid for the horse.

From half a mile away, Jigger distinctly could see the flash of the priceless water as it was poured. He could see the poor horse shake its head with eagerness for more. Then tall Tim Riley fastened the canteen back in its place beside the saddle.

This was the moment that Buzz Mahoney, snatching out a holstered rifle from the other side of the saddle, dropped to his knee and began to pour shot after shot at Jigger.

But Jigger, at a thousand yards, laughed, and the laughter was a dry whisper in his throat.

He took off his hat and waved it, as though in encouragement. And the two remounted, and went on.

VII

For nearly another hour, Jigger traveled in the wake of the pair, and still they seemed to be laboring in vain, never bringing the mountains closer.

Then trouble struck suddenly. They had dismounted to take water and give it to the horse again when Jigger saw by their gestures that they were in a heated argument. Two guns flashed like two dancing bits of blue flame. Then he saw Mahoney fall on his face. Afterward the swift rattle of the reports struck his ear.

Tim Riley mounted and continued on his way, looking back toward the spot where his victim lay.

Jigger, for some reason, looked suddenly up toward the buzzards that wheeled softly in the sky above him. They would be fed, now.

But the figure of Mahoney lifted from the ground. He ran a few steps in pursuit of Riley, and the small sound of his distant wailing came into the ears of Jigger.

To get mercy from Riley was an impossibility that not even the bewildered brain of a wounded man could entertain long. Jigger, with a queer sickness of the heart, saw Mahoney tear the shirt from his back and fall to digging in the sand.

Already the shock and the pain of bullet wounds, the swift loss of blood, and the burning caustic of the heat of Alkali Flat had reduced him to the madness of famine.

Jigger came up rapidly, calling out. He was almost at the point where Mahoney groveled in the sand on his knees, scooping at the earth with his hands, before the wounded man looked up. He saw Jigger with the bewilderment with which he might have stared at a heavenly angel. Then he came with a scream of hope distending his mouth and eyes, his arms thrown out.

Blood ran down his body, which was swollen with strength rather than with fat. But he disregarded his wounds until he had drunk deeply. Then, recovering his wits a little, he looked rather vaguely up to Jigger.

"You're still back on the trail, eh?" said Mahoney. "Leave me ride that other horse, will you?"

"You can ride it if you want," agreed Jigger.

There might have been twenty murders on the hands of this fellow, but still Jigger pitied him.

Mahoney grasped the pommel of the saddle on the led horse, but suddenly weakness overcame him. He looked down with a singular wonder at the blood that rolled down his body. Those wounds were beyond curing, as Jigger had seen at a glance. Mahoney realized it now, also, and the realization struck him down to his knees. He slumped to the side, his mouth open as he dragged at the hot, dusty air.

Jigger, dismounting, kneeled by him.

Mahoney cursed him. "Leave me be. I'm cooked," he said. "Go get Riley. Riley . . . he murdered me. I'm the eleventh man on his list. Him and Mendoza was like a coupla brothers. If I could live to see Riley crawl. . . . But I sure snagged him with my second shot. He's hurt. And them that are hurt in Alkali Flat . . ."

He dropped flat on his back, and Jigger thought that he was gone. But after a moment he spoke again, saying: "He thinks he'll get loose . . . but in Alkali Flat . . . death . . . death . . . will get through a scratch on the skin. Riley . . . Riley . . ."

A little shudder went through him, as though he had been touched by cold.

And Jigger turned to remount, for he knew that Mahoney was dead.

Had Buzz really struck Tim Riley with one of his bullets? It seemed very likely, considering that they had exchanged shots almost hand to hand. And yet Tim Riley was voyaging steadily on across Alkali Flat.

The mountains were closer now. They had lost their blueness entirely and turned brown. Clouds covered the heads of some of the peaks— a paradise of happiness to wander, however blindly, through the cool dampness of a fog like that above. But in Alkali Flat the heat increased. The life was gone from the air, like the taste from overcooked food, but as the sun slanted from a deeper position in the west, a sort of mist seemed to cover the desert. That was the dust, made visible in the slanting sun rays just as the motes grow visible in the sun shaft that strikes through a window in winter. And this film of dust was what made breathing so difficult, perhaps.

Mahoney was dead. A division of the buzzards had dropped toward the ground, but still others trailed after Tim Riley.

Had they scented the death that might even now be working in the body of Riley?

As Mahoney had well said, through the smallest scratch death could enter the bodies of men in Alkali Flat. Where the struggle for mere existence was so hard, the slightest wound, the slightest extra drain on the strength might prove fatal.

Yet Tim Riley, so far as Jigger could see, even through the glass, rode erect and steady.

Jigger closed his thousand yards of safety to a quarter of a mile, to study the gunman. But he had a strong feeling that he was about to lose his long battle. For now the mountains rose like a wall against the sky; the heat of the sun was diminishing; twilight would unroll like a blessing across Alkali Flat before long, and Tim Riley would be among the slopes of the foothills, hunting for the sound of running water in the night, climbing steadily toward a purer, cooler air.

Where the flat ended, Jigger saw the white streak of it just ahead, like a watermark drawn across the hills. And Tim Riley was approaching that mark when, all at once, Jigger saw that the horse was plodding on with downward head, as before, but with an empty saddle.

But no, it was not empty. The rider had slumped well forward and lay out on the neck of the horse.

It might be a bit of playing 'possum, Jigger thought. For Riley must have realized that his pursuer was not armed, and now this might be a device to draw the other into easy range.

So Jigger pressed forward only slowly until he noticed that the buzzards were swaying lower and lower through the air above the head of the fugitive.

As though they conveyed a direct message to him, Jigger lost all fear at once and closed in abruptly.

As he came, he saw the rider slipping slowly, inch by inch, toward the side.

When Jigger came up, he waited until he actually had a hand on the shoulder of Tim Riley before he called out. But Tim Riley continued to lie prone, as though resting from a great fatigue.

He was resting indeed, for he was dead.

When Jigger stopped the horses at the base of the first foothill, he found that Tim Riley had been shot deeply through the body, a wound that might not have been fatal under ordinary circumstances, but which surely meant death in Alkali Flat.

And Riley had known that. He had lashed himself in his saddle. With his hands on the pommel, he had ridden erect, keeping his face toward safety and the mountains.

The mere instinct to keep on fighting had driven him on. A queer admiration crept through the heart of Jigger as he looked at the lean, hard face of Riley, still set and grim and purposeful in death, with a long-distance look in his eyes, as though he were sighting some goal on the great journey on which he was now embarked.

In the saddlebag strapped behind the saddle was what Jigger had struggled and striven so hard to reach.

He knew that but left the thing untouched, while he urged the tired horse up the hill. He walked beside the horse that carried the dead man, to make sure that the body did not slip to the ground. A last, grim hour they struggled up that slope until Jigger heard the sound of running water. A moment later the horses were standing belly-deep in a pool of blue, while Jigger drank and drank again from the rivulet that fed the little lake.

By the side of that lake he buried Tim Riley by the simple device of laying the body under a boulder above which a little slide of rocks was hanging. A few stones moved, and that slide was launched. Fifty tons of débris rushed down over the spot where Riley lay. His funeral oration was the flying echoes that talked and sang busily together for a few seconds all along the cañon.

By the little pool, when it was holding the stars and the thin yellow flickering of the campfire, Jigger ate hard tack, drank coffee, and examined the contents of the big saddlebag.

It was, in fact, the savings of an entire life of crime. He counted, bill by bill, $315,000 of hard cash. In addition, there were a number of jewels, choice stones that had been broken out of their settings.

The blood began to beat fast in the temples of Jigger.

VIII

Levison, president and chief shareholder in the Levison Bank of Tucker Flat, still went down to his office, every day. He carried himself exactly as he had done when the lifting of his finger was enough to control the wild men and the strong men of Tucker Flat.

He had a short, black mustache, his eyebrows and eyes were black but his hair was a thin cloud of white. He was a narrow, tall, straight man who had looked the world in the face for so many years that disaster could not teach him to bow his head. When he walked down the street, now, people scowled at him and they cursed him in audible undertones, but he walked neither more quickly nor more slowly. His wife knew that Levison was dying of a broken heart, but he was dying on his feet.

Every day he went down to the bank, unlocked the front door, walked past the grille work of gilded steel, past the empty cages of the cashier and clerk, and into his own office, where he unlocked his desk and waited.

Sometimes he was there all day, and nothing happened, but often someone entered to talk over the recent robbery and to curse Levison for not guarding the treasures of others more securely.

Levison used to answer: "If there is any fault, it is mine. You have a right to denounce me. No man should dare to fail in this world of ours."

And he kept his chin high, while grief like an inward wolf devoured his heart.

On this day, his walk down the street had been particularly a trial. For the unemployed from the closed mines were thick in the street and they had learned to attribute their lack of a job to the failure of the bank that had shut up the mines. So they thronged thickly about Levison, shook their fists in his face, cursed him and all his ancestors. He went through them like a sleepwalker and never answered a word. Perhaps he hoped that one of the drunkards would strike him down and that the rest would pluck the life out of his body—it was not rooted very deep in his flesh, these days.

When he came to his office, he sat with his head bowed a little and his hands folded together on the edge of his desk. He wanted to die, quickly, but there was that hollow-checked woman who waited for him in the house on the hill from which the servants had been discharged. Wherever she went, even into death, she would follow him not more than a step behind.

He heard the front door of the bank open in the middle of the morning. A step sounded in the emptiness of the big outer room, and then a hand tapped at his door.

"Come in!" called Levison.

The door was pushed open by a slender young fellow with black hair and blue eyes. He was very brown of skin, erect of carriage, and his clothes were mere ragged patches. Over his shoulder he carried a saddlebag.

"Were you a depositor in my bank?" asked Levison, opening the usual formula.

"I never was, but I intend to be," said the stranger.

Levison frowned. "The bank has failed," he said gravely.

"Then we'd better bring it back to life again," said the other.

"Who are you?" snapped Levison.

"Name of Jigger. And here's the stuff that Joe Mendoza and Tim Riley and Buzz Mahoney stole from your vault. All of that and a little more. How much did you lose?"

Levison rose slowly from his chair. He stared into the blue eyes of this young man, and it seemed to him that they were the blue of flame before it turns yellow.

"Two hundred and fifty-two thousand, five hundred and fourteen dollars," he said. That number was written somewhere across his soul as across a parchment.

"Count it out of this lot, then," said Jigger. "There's plenty more. And then tell me where the rest of the cash ought to go . . . or have I claim to it? It's the life savings of Mister Murderer Mendoza!"

At the little shack outside the town of Tucker Flat, big Doc Landy strode back and forth and up and down. Three men waited near the small campfire, never speaking, looking curiously across at Landy now and then.

"I been double-crossed," said Doc Landy. "I ought to send you out on his trail right now. But I'm gonna wait to see has he got the nerve to come here and face me. I'm gonna wait another half hour."

"Hark at them singing!" said one of the men, lifting his head.

For from the town of Tucker Flat there poured distant rumblings and even thin, high-pitched, half-hysterical laughter.

For the bank of Levison had reopened, and the mines that had recovered their deposits were reopening, also. That was reason enough to make the men of Tucker Flat rejoice.

Here there was a slight noise of rustling leaves among the shrubbery, and then into the dimness of the firelight rode a man on a great golden stallion.

"Jigger!" exclaimed Doc Landy.

"Get the three of them out of the way," said Jigger, halting Fanfare.

"Back up, boys," said the peddler. "Wait somewhere . . . somewheres that I can whistle to you."

The three rose, stared an instant at Jigger like dogs marking a quarry, and then stalked away.

Jigger went to the fire, rinsed a tin cup, and filled it with coffee. He made and lit a cigarette to accompany the coffee, and blew the smoke into the air after a deep inhalation.

"Well?" said Landy, growling. "You done yourself fine, I hear?"

"Who told you I did?" asked Jigger.

"Nobody else would've got the money back. Nobody else would've got it back for Levison, and then told him to swear not to use the name. *You* got the money Mendoza stole."

"Levison has his quarter of a million," said Jigger. "And there was something left over. You get half." He took out a sheaf of bills tied about by a piece of string and threw it like a stick of wood to the peddler. "There's a shade over sixty thousand in that," said Jigger. "Count out your half. Besides, there's this stuff. Levison says that I have a right to it. So you take half of this, too . . . seeing that I'm your hired man."

He threw a little chamois sack into the hands of Landy, who lifted his head once, and thrust out his long jaw before he began to reckon the treasure.

After that, he was employed for a long time. At last he looked up and said hoarsely: "Where's Mahoney?"

"In Alkali Flat," said Jigger.

"Dead?"

"Yes."

"Where's Tim Riley?"

"In the hills near Alkali Flat."

"Dead?"

"Yes."

"You let 'em find the stuff, and then you took it away from 'em?"

"Yes."

"And you didn't use a gun?"

"No."

"What *did* you use?"

"The sun and the buzzards," said Jigger.

Landy rubbed a hand back across the bald spot of his head.

"You had the brains to do that . . . and you was still fool enough to turn back a quarter of a million to that Levison?"

Jigger sipped black coffee.

"You don't even get any glory out of it!" shouted Landy. "You won't let Levison tell who done the job for him. There ain't a soul in the world but me that knows what you done!"

"Pop," said Jigger, "glory is a dangerous thing for a fellow like me."

The peddler stared at him. "A hundred and twenty-five thousand to you . . . the same to me . . . and you threw it away! You ain't human! You're a fool!"

298

Jigger sipped more coffee and drew on his cigarette.

"Tell me," growled Doc Landy. "What you expect to get out of life? If you don't want money, what *do* you want?"

"Fun," Jigger said thoughtfully.

"This here hell trail, this here work you done in Alkali Flat that even the birds . . . save the buzzards . . . won't fly over . . . was that fun? Where was the fun in that?"

"The look in the eyes of Levison," Jigger said thoughtfully. "That was the fun for me, Doc."

About the Author

Max Brand is the best-known pen name of Frederick Faust, creator of Dr. Kildare, Destry, and many other fictional characters popular with readers and viewers worldwide. Faust wrote for a variety of audiences in many genres. His enormous output, totaling approximately 30,000,000 words or the equivalent of five hundred and thirty ordinary books, covered nearly every field: crime, fantasy, historical romance, espionage, Westerns, science fiction, adventure, animal stories, love, war, and fashionable society, big business and big medicine. Eighty motion pictures have been based on his work along with many radio and television programs. For good measure he also published four volumes of poetry. Perhaps no other author has reached more people in more different ways. Born in Seattle in 1892, orphaned early, Faust grew up in the rural San Joaquin Valley of California. At Berkeley he became a student rebel and one-man literary movement, contributing prodigiously to all campus publications. Denied a degree because of unconventional conduct, he embarked on a series of adventures culminating in New York City where, after a period of near starvation, he received simultaneous recognition as a serious poet and successful author of fiction. Later, he traveled widely, making his home in New York, then in Florence, and finally in Los Angeles. Once the United States entered the Second World War, Faust abandoned his lucrative writing career and his work as a screenwriter to serve as a war correspondent with the infantry in Italy, despite his fifty-one years and a bad heart. He was killed during a night attack on a hilltop village held by the German army. New books based on magazine serials or unpublished manuscripts or restored versions continue to appear so that, alive or dead, he has averaged a new book every four months for seventy-five years. Beyond this, some work by him is newly reprinted every week of every year in one or another format somewhere in the world. A great deal more about this author and his work can be found in *The Max Brand Companion* (Greenwood Press, 1997) edited by Jon Tuska and Vicki Piekarski. His Website is www.MaxBrandOnline.com.

Additional Copyright Information

Center Point Large Print
600 Brooks Road / PO Box 1
Thorndike, ME 04986-0001 USA

(207) 568-3717

US & Canada:
1 800 929-9108
www.centerpointlargeprint.com